The Billionaire Bum

A Novel by K. D. Fleeger

ISBN   1453712089
EAN-13   9781453712085

"We think sometimes that poverty is only being hungry, naked and homeless. The poverty of being unwanted, unloved and uncared for is the greatest poverty."

- Mother Teresa

Prologue

Jackson Hayes, brilliant real estate tycoon, entrepreneur and financial genius, was walking home from work. Admittedly, this was a rare event prompted by the early springtime weather coupled with an extremely irritating late-afternoon meeting.

He was in the process of purchasing a company owned by none other than Mr. Nicholas Carver, a shrewd businessman who had repeatedly made appearances in Jackson's life, much to Jackson's dismay. Nick seemed untrustworthy and never failed to set Jackson's teeth on edge, but his company did appear to be a good investment. The board of Hayes Enterprises was pushing for this acquisition despite their young CEO's doubts. The due diligence checked out, and pending any further information, the deal was scheduled to close in less than thirty days.

Jackson loosened his tie and threw his perfectly tailored jacket over his arm for the hike across town. He was looking down at his over-priced PDA and absentmindedly running his fingers through his disheveled hair.

Half a block ahead a retired Vietnam war veteran who had

come across some rather hard times lately was sitting on the sidewalk stretching the muscles in his right leg, and holding a cup for change. Some aches, it seemed, never went away.

Perhaps if Jackson had looked up, he might have noticed the man sitting on the sidewalk with his legs outstretched, but as it was, he literally stumbled right over him. A startled, "What the...?" escaped his lips before he scraped one palm against the sidewalk and managed to right himself. The man that he had tripped over tumbled sideways, spilling loose change from his cup.

"Watch where the hell you're going," he growled, frantically collecting the spilled coins.

"Don't sit in the middle of the fucking sidewalk," Jackson spat in return.

"Fucking self-absorbed asshole..." The man's mumbled sentence faded off as he righted himself and went back to shaking his cup.

Jackson could have simply ignored the man and went on his way with no further thought, but this day had been frustrating enough, without adding insult to injury from a filthy street bum, and Jackson had never been one to back down from a fight. Before he knew it, the argument was falling from his lips.

"What did you call me? Self-absorbed? Fucking self-absorbed? That's rich coming from a man with no work ethic who doesn't even pay taxes. You're a fucking drain on the system, and you think I'm selfish. At least I take care of myself. What the fuck have you ever done?"

The homeless man stood slowly, ignoring the pain that the action caused, and looked Jackson dead in the eye. Our dear Mr. Hayes couldn't have known it, but this man had seen far worse in his sixty-odd-years than the likes of a uptight businessman. Where Jackson expected to see shame he instead saw perseverance. These were the eyes of one who never gives up, no matter how broken.

"You've been handed everything your whole life, pretty boy. You wouldn't survive one week living like me."

The man turned and limped away down the street, leaving a speechless Jackson alone on the sidewalk.

Jackson's phone vibrated in his hand, pulling him out of his stunned silence.

"Hello," he answered coldly.

"What's up, my brother?" Jason's boisterous voice echoed through the phone.

"Nothing."

"Good, we're having a night out. Shelby is off at some fashion show thing, and you know I can't cook for shit. I'll meet you at the Phyrst in half an hour."

The line went dead.

Jackson looked up at the street sign. He was still ten blocks from home, and it was a ten-minute drive from home to the bar. It looked like he'd need that cab after all.

The Bet

Jackson

I felt decidedly better after a change of clothes and draught lager. My brother Jason had a natural ability to cure me of whatever funk I might be in, and I found myself very glad that he had called me out for burgers and beer. We'd been comparing our days back and forth for the last few minutes.

"..so then the guy has the audacity to call me a self-absorbed asshole," I said. "Can you believe that? When he's the one practically lying in the middle of the street?"

Jason chuckled and shook his head, taking a long swig of his beer.

"And then," I continued. "And then, when I called him on it, he tells me that I wouldn't survive one week in his shoes. It's like he thinks being a bum is hard work or something."

I paused while the waitress set our burgers in front of us. "This looks so good. I was freaking starving."

Jason was still shaking his head and laughing across the table. "He's right though," he said.

"Who's right?"

"The bum. I mean being homeless is hard. I sure as hell wouldn't want to try it."

"What?" I paused with my burger halfway to my mouth. "You think sitting in the middle of the damn street all day is difficult?"

"Well no, man," Jason said, "but it's no picnic either. You know how much I eat, and I wouldn't want to be worried about where the next meal was coming from all the time."

I smiled at my brother. He wasn't kidding. The man had two burgers and a huge pile of fries in front of him right now, but I knew that they wouldn't last long. Jason was built like a tank. He stood six foot six and was known to fill an entire doorway with his broad shoulders. He could pack away food like no other.

"Well yeah," I agreed, "but you could just get a part-time job in a burger joint and you'd be set. I'm sure you could eat all the customer rejects." I watched as he shoveled a few more fries into his mouth. "I mean why don't those people just get jobs and stop bothering the rest of us who are willing to put in a decent day's work?"

Jason's face took on a tone of seriousness that I wasn't really accustomed to. "I don't know, man. I don't think it's that simple. I mean, would you hire a homeless guy?"

"Well, of course not, Jason, but we're in business acquisitions. There has to be some kind of more appropriate employment for these guys, like manual labor type stuff."

"I don't think so, Bro. I'm not saying that I like being pestered by them out on the street begging, but I think living a week as a homeless person would be hard. I'd give you about twelve hours out there with no credit cards, and I bet you'd have a lot more sympathy for them."

"No way." My brother was looking at me like I'd grown two heads. "There is no fucking way that I would just give up like that. If I were homeless, I would find a way to work to better myself. No way in hell would I settle for begging in the street. I would fare so much better than any of these lousy drains on society."

Jason smiled his typical, huge, goofy smile at me, and I knew that I was in trouble.

"Fine man," he said. "I've got $50,000 that says you can't last one week as a homeless dude."

"What?" I asked, my burger long forgotten.

"You heard me." He was fucking laughing at me now. "I'll bet you fifty grand that you don't make it one week going homeless. You leave here tonight and give me your keys, your credit cards, everything. Hell, I'll even let you keep the cash that's in your wallet and your driver's license, which is probably more than most homeless guys start off with. One week from today, I'll give it all back to you, if you don't come begging to me to have it all back before then."

"You can't be fucking serious," I said. "I'm in the middle of closing the Carver deal. I can't just take off to go be homeless for a week."

"Sure you can," he said. "When was the last time you took a vacation? I'll tell everyone you had the sudden urge to see Hawaii. You and I both know that you're spending too much time stressing over that deal anyway. The board already made the decision. The deal will close just fine without you, and even if it doesn't, you didn't want to buy the damn company in the first place."

He was right. I was usually very heavily involved in the beginning and ending stages of an acquisition, but there was always a little lag time while the lawyers fought with each other when my presence wasn't strictly necessary.

It had been a long time since I'd had a break from my ordinary routine. Jason and I used to pull crazy shit like this all the time in college. It had been too long. Maybe this would be fun.

"Deal," I said. "Fifty thousand dollars says I'm perfectly fine at the end of one week of being homeless."

Bodyguards and The First Night

Jason

"No, I just need you to follow him around at night. Just make sure he doesn't get his ass killed," I said.

Ben was cracking up on the other end of the line. "You want me to follow your dumb-ass brother around for a week while he's pretending to be homeless? You rich people are so damn weird."

"Shut up, man. Just tell me you'll do it."

"Yeah," he said, "I'll babysit him for you, but you're paying me for the whole week even if he quits early."

"Sure thing. Thanks, Ben." I flipped my phone shut and put my head in my hands. Shel would probably kick my ass when she found out what I'd done.

Jackson had totally gone off the deep end on me. I know the stupid bet was my idea, but I didn't actually expect him to take me up on it. Dude clearly had no sense of self-preservation. He'd be lucky to not get his ass killed in the first twenty-four hours.

So, I called Ben as soon as I got home. Someone had to

watch him to make sure that he didn't really get into too much trouble. Ben and I had played college football together. He was almost as big as I was. We'd stayed in touch periodically, and I knew that he was still in the area. Ben worked in the security business as a personal bodyguard and had more common sense than most people. I knew that he wouldn't let anything really bad happen to my brother.

Jackson had almost seventy dollars on him when I left him, and he'd just eaten, so he wouldn't starve over night. I just hoped that he wouldn't get himself shot or beaten to death. This was a pretty safe city, all things considered, but he wasn't exactly the picture of street smart. This was going to be a real learning experience for him.

One night on the streets might even be good for him - teach him a little humility. I'd be the first to admit that we were both born with silver spoons in our mouths. I'm not sure that Jackson ever really understood how blessed we were. As much as I loved my brother, I could admit that he had a sense of entitlement about him that had always bugged me. Grades, money, women - everything came easily for him. He hadn't been told "no" very often in his life, but that was all right. He was amazing at his job, and for the most part I thought he was pretty happy with life, but there were times, like last night, when I thought he'd really lost touch with the world. He could get so caught up in the stressful details of his own shit that he missed the big picture completely.

Who was I to judge, though? I could be like that, too. *Thank you, God, for sending me Shelby.* That woman had a way of grounding me and setting my ass straight. Jackson needed a woman like that.

Jackson

So what the hell am I going to do now?

I really hadn't thought this through the whole way. If I had, I probably would have insisted on waiting until morning to start this ridiculous nonsense. I could have had one more good night's sleep in my own bed. I also would have dressed a little more appropriately. As it was, I was wearing designer jeans, a plain grey t-shirt and light spring jacket. I wasn't exactly planning on tenting out for the week. I guess it could have been worse though, at least I had changed out of my suit.

First order of business: find a place to bed down for the night.

I ran a list of possibilities through my head. I knew that this city had homeless shelters somewhere, but of course I had no idea where they might be, and I couldn't Google it because Jason took my iPhone. The thought of a shelter didn't really appeal to me anyway, but it was better than staying outside. It still got pretty cold at night in the spring. Of course, the doorman for my own building knew me. I owned the whole place and paid his salary. I could get into my penthouse apartment without my keys, if I really wanted to, but I was no cheater, and I had a feeling that Jason would find out somehow if I did go home.

Could I find a hotel cheap enough? That was probably a bad idea. I needed to put myself on a budget. I had about ten dollars a day if I wanted to last the week. A hotel that cost less than fifty bucks a night wasn't exactly my idea of fun anyway.

So that left public places where you could sleep without being noticed or bothered. The subway was good thought. I knew I'd seen homeless people camped out there. It was still cold though, and I was hoping for somewhere warmer. The airport? I didn't have any luggage, but I was well enough dressed with my three hundred dollar shoes, and I thought I could pass for a traveler waiting for an early morning transfer. No one brought carry-on luggage anymore anyway, right? It was too much of a security pain.

That seemed like the best idea. I'd come up with a better plan for tomorrow night, but it was already creeping up on midnight, and I was ready to lie down for a while.

It was only about twenty minutes to the airport by subway and the trip passed quickly despite my dislike of public transportation. The ticket cost eight dollars, but it was good for three days anywhere on the whole subway system. I had a feeling that mobility might be important in this game.

The airport was pretty dead this time of night. Most of the shops and restaurants were closed and only a small handful of employees were left at the ticket counters checking-in late night passengers. I found a vacant set of three chairs linked together in the hallway around the corner from the United Airlines check-in counter. The bathrooms were right across the hall, and I was just out of sight of the security line. Perfect.

I balled up my jacket and slipped it under my head as a makeshift pillow. It wouldn't be the best night's sleep I'd ever had, but I thought I probably would get some sleep, and that was good enough for now.

Morning Dawns on a Man for Hire

Jackson

"Wake up, sir."

"What?" I mumbled, shielding my eyes from the blinding fluorescent light.

Where the hell am I?

"I need to see your boarding pass and driver's license."

A police officer? No, he was a security guard. Airport security. I wondered how long I had been asleep.

"Oh, I'm sorry," I mumbled, trying to shake off the sleep. "I um…"

I didn't have a boarding pass. I wasn't flying anywhere. I was camping out in the airport because of some stupid-ass bet I'd made with my brother. *How many beers did I have before agreeing to this?*

"I haven't checked-in for my flight yet," I said stupidly. "Could you tell me what time it is?"

"It's almost four a.m.," he said. "You can't stay here without a boarding pass. Check-in for your flight and go through security. You can sleep at the gates but not out here."

"Oh," I said. "Yeah, my flight leaves in about two hours anyway, I guess. So I'll go do that now." He looked at my doubtfully but didn't press any further.

Barely three hours of sleep.

I ducked into the bathroom to wash my face. Getting a toothbrush was definitely on the agenda for today. My hair was a disheveled mess, even more so than usual, and I had developed a kink in my neck from the uncomfortable sleeping position. It would be dark for at least two and half more hours. What on earth was I going to do until morning? I clearly couldn't stay here, as I'd just lied to the security guard.

I left the bathroom and walked down to the subway platform. The cold night air crept in here, and the cement tunnel felt eerily deserted. I sat on one of the cold wooden benches and waited for the train.

I wanted a cigarette.

I hadn't smoked since college, and even then, I only smoked when I drank. Funny how being awake at four in the morning gave me that craving.

Eight minutes later the subway screeched to a stop, and I climbed aboard the empty car. I chose a seat in the back corner and laid my head against the window. This train was on a loop from the airport to downtown. I'd taken it occasionally when I was traveling without a lot of luggage. I preferred to leave my cars in the garage at home where I knew that they'd be safe. Who knows what could happen to a car left unattended in the airport parking lot?

Supposedly, the train would just continue to make the loop every forty minutes or so, twenty-four hours a day. There wasn't a lot of traffic going to and from the airport right now, so I thought my seat would remain mostly unoccupied with the possible exception of the four downtown stops. I knew it wouldn't be great, but my body was not ready to give up on sleep yet, and I didn't want to wander the streets until daylight.

If I made the loop three times, it should get me through until morning.

I was really going to have to make better arrangements for tonight. I began putting a list together in my head. First things first, I would find a job. I was not a lazy homeless bum. I would work my way into a better sleeping place for tonight.

I knew that I'd have to find someone who would pay me a daily. If I had to wait a week for my first paycheck, the whole thing would be a moot point. Surely, someone would need day labor.

I slept fitfully. The first loop was all right, but as it grew closer to morning the subway became more and more crowded and sleep became less possible. It was difficult to keep track of time in an underground world, but I finally decided to make my exit when I could see daylight filtering down the stairwell at one of the stops.

I wearily left my seat and climbed out into the heart of downtown. It was raining... of course. I reminded myself that it could have been worse; it could have been snow. I hoped that I wouldn't get too soaked.

I stopped at a newsstand and picked up a paper. I needed the help wanted section, and I was hoping that I might be able to find a charitable organization that would let me sleep in temporary housing for a few days.

I stepped out of the rain and into a small breakfast café that was just opening for business. Despite the burger last night, I was hungry. My body seemed to be burning more calories from the lack of sleep. I ordered coffee and a short stack of pancakes. $6.50. I wasn't accustomed to eating on a budget. After leaving a tip, I would be down to almost $50. I was going to need an income in a hurry.

Help wanted. Administrative Assistant, Sales, Real Estate, Dish Washer – that was a possibility, Bar Tender – that would mean immediate tips, but I wondered if I would need training. I could pull pints of beer, but I wasn't too sure about all the crazy mixed drinks.

Well, it was a place to start anyway.

Now for shelter – where would they put the listings for homeless shelters and temporary housing? Classifieds maybe? I searched the paper from cover to cover and found no information on shelters. How were you supposed to find these places? Through a church? *Maybe.*

I hadn't been in a church since Jason's wedding almost four years ago.

I left a small tip for the waitress and then headed back out into the rain, only mildly satisfied by my pancakes. The bar probably wouldn't open until noon, so I'd have to wait to inquire about the bar-tending job. In the meantime, I was in need of a toothbrush and some deodorant. Who knew that it would take less than a day to feel this disgusting? Between the subway grime and the light rain, I was feeling dirty already, and I didn't think that was the best way to go job hunting.

The RiteAid down the street proved helpful. I bought a toothbrush, travel toothpaste, travel deodorant and a bar of soap. I paid for them and then carried my bag to the restroom in the back of the store. I locked the door and pulled my shirt over my head. Getting cleaned up in a public bathroom wasn't ideal, but I thought it would do for now. I did feel a lot better knowing that at least my teeth were clean.

There were several churches between the RiteAid and the bar, so I thought I'd stop and ask for information on shelters and possibly soup kitchens. I couldn't keep eating out, unless I found a source of income. My cash was dwindling quickly.

The first two churches appeared to be locked. Seriously? Who locked a church? Didn't they have office staff that would be around during the day or something? The third church was also a Catholic school. This one had unlocked doors, but the administrative assistants that I came across were only associated with the school and could offer me no assistance with homeless ministries.

On the fourth try, I managed to find a back entrance that admitted me to a pastor's office. There was a woman sitting behind a cheap desk, her eyes focused intently on the bulky computer screen. After a moment, I cleared my throat, hoping that she would acknowledge me. She looked up quickly as if I had startled her.

"Can I help you?" she asked, never ceasing her typing.

"Uh, yeah," I replied, "I was hoping that you might able to help me find some information on homeless shelters."

"You'll have to be a bit more specific." She was looking at me like I was daft.

"I just wanted to know where the homeless shelters or soup kitchens might be located in the city and also their hours of operation if you have it."

Her eyes raked up and down my body as if considering why I would want such information. I knew that I wasn't looking my best, but I hardly looked homeless.

"Do you want to make a donation?"

Good. That meant that I didn't look like a bum, at least not to her.

"Well, possibly," I said, which was mostly true. I would consider making a donation, if I could find a place that would help me get through the rest of the week with my pride intact. "But I wanted to see the places first. I prefer to take a personal interest in the charities that I support."

"Mmhmmm," she replied, "well, there is a battered woman's shelter three blocks up on Shady Avenue." That wasn't going to help me, as they didn't allow men. "And a men's shelter over on 5th. They have a drug rehab, too." That was more promising, although the thought of spending the night with drug addicts was less than appealing. "And I know there's a soup kitchen at Grace Evangelical, but I think it's only on Fridays. I'm not sure if someone would be there during the rest of the week. I'm afraid that's all the information I have. If you want to make a donation though, I'm sure I could get it into the right hands for you."

"No, thank you," I said, "but I appreciate the information."

I left the office and wandered back into the rain. I would wait until the bar opened, apply for the job, and then head over to the men's shelter. If all else failed, I could make a few friends amongst my "peers" in the shelter who might be able tell me where to find a decent free meal.

It was just after 10:30 am when I reached the bar that had posted the ad in the paper. Sure enough, there was a help wanted sign in the window as well.

I knew that there was work available for those who weren't lazy. Some people just need to get off their asses.

The hours posted on the door said they would open at 11:00.

Having time to kill was an unusual experience for me. I was itching to check my email or at least place a call to my personal assistant. Time moved so much slower outside of the corporate world.

There was a small park across the street with a fountain and couple of park benches. It was an appealing place to sit and wait. The rain had stopped temporarily, but the benches were still wet. I wiped the rain off as best I could and then perched precariously on the driest edge of the seat. I unfolded my newspaper in front of me. If the bar-tending job didn't pan out, I would try the dishwasher next. It was on the way to the shelter anyway.

Maybe I could get some lunch, too. Those pancakes weren't holding me.

Finally, a middle-aged man stepped out from the bar and unlocked the door. I walked across the street.

"Good morning, sir," I said, extending my hand. "My name is Jackson. I was hoping to apply for your open bartending position."

He shook my hand and let his eyes sweep over my form. I was hoping that I looked young enough to pass for a recently graduated college student. "I'll give you an application," he said.

I sat at the bar and filled out the application with a

borrowed pen. Permanent address. Well that was going to be a problem. I couldn't exactly tell him that I lived in the penthouse suite of the highest-priced apartment building in this city. I had other homes as well: a beach house off the coast of South America, and a ski chalet in Tahoe, but neither of those would work for this application. Could I list my parent's address? I wrote it down.

Phone number. Shit. Jason had my phone. If an employer wanted to call me, I would be virtually unreachable.

Work history. Yeah, I'm the CEO of one of the most profitable companies in the United States. I was clearly going to have to edit my work history.

Fuck, this is going to be impossible.

I finally settled for making everything up. I gave my parent's phone number. I was going to pretend to be still living at their home, but I would have to do everything that I could to keep him from calling their house. I could just hear my mother now, "Why is my son applying for a job at a bar? Are you sure he didn't want to buy your bar? Would you consider it an investment property?" That would not be good. I was going to have to talk my way out of this before it came to calling anyone.

I can do this.

I was a Princeton graduate for God's sake. Of course, my application named a local state system university instead, but somehow I didn't think that it would matter for a position pouring drinks. Surely, I could bullshit my way through one lousy interview.

"Sir?" I said, putting on my most professional and respectful demeanor. "I've finished the application. I was hoping that you might have time to conduct an interview now, if everything looks acceptable, of course."

He took my application and skimmed it briefly. "You've never tended bar before?"

"No, sir. But I did work in a pizza shop for a while where

we served beer."

It was a lie. I had interned with a large commercial real estate firm for a year when I was in college. That was the closest I'd ever come to this line of work, which wasn't very close. He gave me a non-committal grunt. I was going to have to do something in a hurry or this interview was going to go downhill fast.

Just then the door opened and two beautiful young women stepped through. The bar was open for lunch and the two of them, probably co-workers, appeared to be here for sandwiches and possibly cocktails. I could do this. I put on my very best smile and then turned to my new customers.

"Hi, come on in," I said, throwing the full weight of my inherited Hayes charm at them. I grabbed a couple of menus from the bar and ushered them to a table. The owner hadn't stopped me yet, and I was too afraid to look over my shoulder for his approval. I handed the girls the menus. "What can I get you lovely ladies to drink?"

One of them giggled and one of them blushed. Yes! Even homeless I could charm the pants off of them. I allowed myself a brief moment to finish that fantasy before they answered.

"Captain and Coke," the first one said. I looked to the other.

"I'll have a Bud Light in a bottle please."

"Coming right up," I said.

I turned back to my interviewer. "Captain and Coke and a Bud Light in a bottle?"

He burst out laughing. "Yeah, all right, smart ass," he said. "The beer is in the cooler in the corner. Captain's right here, and Coke is in the tap." He handed me a glass, pointed to the ice and then showed me how to measure and pour the drink. "Give the girls their drinks and get their order. Then we'll work out the terms."

I did as he asked and was on my way fifteen minutes later, a new employee of the 31st Street Bar and Grill. My new employer's name was Buddy, or at least that's what he said that everyone called him. It was perfect. I was starting tomorrow night. My hours were going to be 8pm to 2am. I thought could survive for the rest of the week on the tips that I would make. I wasn't worried about the hourly paycheck; by the time I would get it, I would be back to my old life anyway.

There was only one small problem. He said that I needed to bring my social security card before he could put me to work. I had one, of course, but it was in my apartment, out of reach. I was going to have to have a new one issued from the social security office. I didn't know where that was, but with any luck it would be between here and the men's shelter.

Things were definitely looking up.

When it All Falls Down

Jackson

I had no idea that payphones still existed, but apparently they did. I located one outside of a convenience store that had about three quarters of a tattered phone book still attached. A quick search, although not as fast as Google, and I had an address for the social security office. It was not within walking distance, and unfortunately nowhere near the shelter, but I still had my subway pass so it was accessible.

My stomach was grumbling, but I wanted to make sure that I had my employment and sleeping place all squared away before taking any more time off today. Skipping lunch probably wouldn't kill me. Jason was right though; food was a definite concern with this lifestyle.

I found the social security office with little trouble and took a number from the machine. The electronic counter on the wall said 26. My number was 34. That didn't seem so bad.

An hour later the number on the wall was 31. I was still 34.

An hour later the number on the wall said 33. I was next, and I was impatient.

Where the hell are all of my tax dollars going? This is ridiculous. No one should have to wait this long for anything.

"Number 34," the woman behind the glass called. Finally!

"Yes," I said. "I need to get a copy of my social security card, please."

"I need a driver's license, birth certificate, and a personal check for $36," she said.

"Um," I stuttered, "I... here's my ID. And I can give you cash?"

I hadn't really meant for that to sound like a question. *Shit. How was I going to pay for this?* I needed that card to be able to work, but I needed to hang on to my money. This was going to wipe me out.

"And, um, I don't have my birth certificate on me..."

"Well, you need to get a copy of your birth certificate, and we don't take cash. It has to be a check or a money order for thirty-six dollars even."

"Where exactly do I get a copy of my birth certificate?" I asked, trying to keep the anger from my voice. I knew it wasn't her fault that the rules were stupid, but could no one have told me this before I waited for over two hours?

"Department of Health, Center for Health Statistics. It's in the courthouse," she said automatically, as if she gave this information two hundred times a day. Which, come to think of it, she probably did. But the courthouse! The damn courthouse was all the way back over by the bar.

"Do you know what a copy of your birth certificate costs?" I asked.

"No idea," she said. She pushed a button and the number on the wall flipped over to 35. "Number 35."

I had clearly been dismissed.

"Wait, but are you sure?!" I pleaded. "There's nothing you can do without a birth certificate?" I gave her the best puppy dog eyes I could possibly muster, and she simply shook her head and looked to the next person in line.

Shit. I looked in my wallet as I stepped on to the street. I had $42.34. I needed $36 for the social security card, plus the fee for getting a money order because they wouldn't take cash, which I thought would probably be a dollar or so. So that left me about $5 with which to buy a birth certificate, dinner, and hopefully a meal tomorrow before my first shift at the bar. Somehow, I didn't think that was going to work.

I was going to have to prioritize. Without the job, I would be screwed for the rest of the week, but getting the job was going to cost me more than I had. I needed to know how much more. I got on the subway again.

When I got to the courthouse, I was forced to take another number, but I had learned my lesson the last time. Instead of sitting idle, I went over to the rack of forms and attempted to decipher the requirements for gaining a birth certificate. I needed form 103-B, a driver's license (man was I glad that Jason let me keep mine), and a check or money order for $20.00.

Well, it could be worse.

I left the courthouse and went across the street to the post office to have the money order made. I now had $21.74 in my wallet, but I was one step closer to a job.

They still hadn't called my number when I returned, but thankfully this line was not as long as the other.

The birth certificate proved to be easier than I thought. I was afraid that there could be a waiting period, but they were able to print me a copy while I waited.

It was now 4:30 pm. I knew that I couldn't make it back to the social security office by 5:00, and even if I could, I was short sixteen dollars. It seemed more logical to head over to the shelter.

Perhaps I could borrow the money from one of the shelter

workers if I explained the situation. I could pay it back as soon as I got my tips the following night.

Ben

I had to give him some credit. Jackson hadn't given up yet. Granted, he hadn't come across any real trouble yet either. I hoped his luck would hold out.

I'd started following him last night as soon as Jason had called. Jason thought it was likely that he would head out to the airport. Apparently, it was one of the places that Jackson felt most comfortable, and Jason was right. We'd found him there, asleep, about an hour before the security guard woke him.

Once you lost a subject it was much harder to find them again, which meant that we were working around the clock. I had Sean, another bodyguard, following him during the day, and I was taking the night shift.

I'd placed a few phone calls today and had gotten a full report on the homeless scene. Fortunately, my work didn't usually require spending the night in shelters and eating in soup kitchens, but I knew from past experiences the right questions to ask. I'd gone through enough rough patches in my life to understand what it meant to be uprooted and alone in a city. It was not easy, but it was manageable if you could establish a routine that involved eating at least once a day, sleeping somewhere safe, and staying out of the elements.

According to Sean's report, Jackson had actually done really well today. He'd found a bar-tending job and gotten a copy of his birth certificate. He'd need a social security card to be able to work, unless he found someone who was willing to pay him under the table. If he was able to work, he might just make it through the week. He was more resourceful than I'd given him credit for – I thought for sure he'd spend the first night in a cheap hotel and go home as soon as he realized that there were cockroaches in the tub.

What concerned me now, however was the subway stop. I'd been sitting four rows behind Jackson on the subway talking with Sean, but after he'd finished his report he headed off home leaving me to follow Jackson alone. Sean hadn't been sure where he was headed. He knew that Jackson had gone into a couple of churches earlier, but he hadn't heard the conversations that took place indoors, so we weren't sure what information he had obtained. We thought that it was safe to assume that he was looking for a place to spend the night, most likely a homeless shelter. There were four in the city. Unfortunately, the subway stop where he was now exiting was only close to one of them, and it was the worst possible choice.

Homeless shelters were usually unsafe at best and could sometimes be downright dangerous. Most shelters would turn you away if you appeared to be high, severely intoxicated, or likely to stir up trouble for another reason. This one did not.

For someone like Jackson, coming here was like begging for trouble.

Would he know that? I doubted it. I didn't think that he would have had any reason to visit this place in the past. Shelters weren't usually on the radar of the extremely wealthy. The Hayes were good people. They gave a lot of money to a lot of good organizations. But, they were the type to hand over large checks at fund-raising banquets, not the type who volunteered to scrub toilets in homeless shelters.

My fears were realized when Jackson pulled on the locked shelter doors. This was going to be a long night.

I stayed out front and watched him walk up the alley looking for a back door. If he found one, it would be locked as well. Everyone planning to stay the night in the shelter would line up in front of the building starting around 7:30 in the evening. They would let the homeless guys in around 8:30. Lights out at 10:00. A privileged few would manage to get into the showers before lights out. The rest would try in the morning before they were evicted. Only about a third of the guys would actually get a shower. During the colder months the shelters would be packed full. They would still be crowded this time of year, but some people would prefer sleeping outside to being here, even if it did get down to about forty-five degrees at night.

Many of Jackson's soon to be bunk-mates were eating at a church about six blocks from here, but Jackson didn't know that. He had to be getting hungry by now. Sean said that he hadn't eaten anything but pancakes all day.

When dinner was finished at the church, the homeless would congregate here in front of the shelter until they were allowed inside. We had about fifteen minutes to go until Jackson would encounter his first taste of what real homeless people were like.

He circled the building. When he didn't find another open entrance he walked to the end of the block and back as if verifying that he was in the right place. A few minutes later the first man showed up with a plastic shopping bag under one arm. He ignored Jackson and shuffled back and forth in front of the shelter steps.

I pulled up the hood of my sweatshirt and moved closer. I doubted that Jackson would recognize me. We'd only met one time, and it had been several years ago. We were also at Jason's wedding together, but we didn't speak to each other as there were about seven hundred people in attendance, including half the politicians in the state. The Hayes family knew how to throw a great party.

I wanted to be close enough to save Jackson's ass should he get into a fight, but far enough away to keep my cover. Jason had made the rules pretty clear to me. "Don't let him get killed, but don't help his ass either." I chuckled under my breath. Jason was a riot.

That meant, though, that I couldn't give Jackson the information that he needed. He was going to have to learn how to communicate with the homeless if he wanted to keep eating. It took a few minutes before Jackson even noticed that people were beginning to congregate in the street. He appeared to be in his own little world. That seemed pretty on par from what I knew of the guy – nice enough, but clearly self-centered.

Finally, he wandered over to a group of three guys who had all come together. I was fairly certain that they had walked up from the soup kitchen as a group. Homeless people had needs that went beyond food and shelter. Humans are pack animals. We all feel the need for social interaction, although some more than others.

"Is this shelter open tonight?" Jackson asked the guys.

They appraised him for a few seconds before one of them spoke up. "Yeah. They open up 'bout eight-thirty."

"Great." Jackson smiled at them, and I had to stuff my fist in my mouth to keep from laughing. He clearly was not accustomed to making small talk with bums. He looked like he was about to hit them with a sales pitch. "Do you guys know where I could get some dinner?"

"You ain't been around long have you?" another one of the guys mumbled. I think he was missing at least half of his teeth, so it came out as a mostly jumbled mess.

"Uh, no," said Jackson. "I just recently… sort of… had well, uh… this is new to me."

"I'll say," laughed the guy who had spoken originally. "But you just missed dinner. On Wednesday it's at the church on Maple."

"Oh," Jackson was clearly disappointed. I wondered if this was the longest he'd ever gone without food. "What about Thursdays? Is there food somewhere tomorrow?"

The three guys looked at each other, and I thought for a minute that they might lie to him and send him on a wild soup kitchen chase, but after a pretty lengthy pause one of them offered up the truth. "Yeah, the Presbyterian Church by the docks. It's at noon."

"Noon. By the docks," Jackson repeated. He was shifting nervously from foot to foot. I was sure he was tired. The guy was used to sitting in meetings all day. He'd done a lot of walking and not a lot of eating. His body was working overtime. He was still incredibly clean compared to most of the guys who were now in line, but his fancy ass jeans were starting to show a little wear, and his hair looked dirtier than usual. If he didn't find a change of clothes soon, he would start to look homeless.

Jackson kept to himself until they opened the shelter doors. He was close to the head of the line so he had a pretty good choice of sleeping space. The building used to be a convent, so there was a long hall with dorm-like rooms on each side that could house six guys in three sets of bunk beds. There was also an open area with four rows of ten cots. I waited to see where he would go before choosing my own space. He chose a top bunk in one of the smaller rooms. It wasn't a bad choice, but the more private rooms were often out of the view of the shelter employees, which meant that there was a higher likelihood of theft. I would be surprised if Jackson made it through the night with his jacket still in his possession.

Sean thought he still had some money on him, and I hoped he had the sense to hide it. Down his pants would be the best place, but Jackson didn't strike me as the type to favor putting cash in his Italian silk boxers.

I took the top bunk on the other side of the room. There was a bed separating us, which would hide me well enough, but still allow me to watch over him.

Now came the tricky part. If he left to use the bathrooms, he would most likely lose his sleeping space. If he didn't get in line now, he wouldn't get a shower. He was observing the line forming at the bathrooms across the way, but he was also watching the other men in our room protect their sleeping spaces. I could tell he was conflicted.

He must have decided that sleep was more important than showering at this point, and I thought he made the right choice. If his luck held, he might be able to get a shower in the morning before heading out. At that point, protecting his sleeping space wouldn't matter.

A shelter worker was making rounds and Jackson called

him over. They had a short conversation and while I couldn't hear it word for word, I got the basic idea. Jackson had asked him to borrow some money - twenty dollars, I think. The young volunteer had quickly and efficiently turned him down.

Rule number one of volunteering in a shelter: never give money to people who were likely to spend it on drugs and then harass you for more. There was no such thing as "borrowing" in a place like this.

Jackson lay down on his bunk when the kid walked away. I couldn't see what he was doing from here, but I thought he was probably rearranging his few possessions. Maybe he did realize the theft potential. I certainly hoped so.

I studied the four other men in the room. The two guys in the middle bunk appeared to be friends, maybe even brothers. One was guarding both beds while the other headed off to the bathrooms. They would likely switch before lights out. I didn't see them as particularly threatening.

In the bunk below my own was an old-timer. He had to be at least seventy years old and looked more like ninety. Homeless people rarely lived past seventy-five or so. This life was hard on the body. He had already put his back to the wall, closed his eyes, and gone to sleep. I thought a man like that could probably sleep anywhere.

The guy who had taken up residence below Jackson had me worried. He had taken a good long look at Jackson before choosing his bunk. He was fairly young, maybe thirty, and I could smell the booze on him from the other side of the room. His eyes were red and bloodshot, and he had a crooked nose that had probably been broken more than a couple of times. He would need to be watched.

Luckily, I had slept for most of the day, because there was no way I would be able to let my guard down in here. The last of the stragglers were coming in now and nearly every bed was full. The last additions were the type that I had been worried about. The main room was getting rowdy as the first fight of the night broke out. A crazy drunk was screaming obscenities about someone who had supposedly cut in the shower line.

Jackson watched with wide-eyed fascination as the shelter workers made him go back to his cot and settle down. They turned off the water to the showers a few minutes later, much to the disappointment of the men still standing in line, and a few minutes after that, the lights went out.

Let the games begin.

Within an hour the place had quieted down. You could hear some loud snoring coming from various parts of the building. There were no doors on the smaller rooms so the sounds echoed down the hall easily. I hadn't heard a peep out of Jackson, so he was either asleep or trying to be.

I flipped open my cell phone to check the time. Almost midnight.

At 12:15 another fight broke out in the main room. It was hard to know exactly what had happened, but it was probably a theft gone awry. It usually was. The shelter workers broke it up and threw both parties out into the night.

A little while later, someone started throwing up. God, what an awful noise that was.

And still, not a peep from Jackson. His downstairs neighbor had been quiet too, but I didn't think I was lucky enough for that to last.

Finally around four o'clock my prediction came true. The guy below Jackson sat up and put his feet very quietly on the floor. I lifted my torso enough so that I could watch, but I didn't leave my bunk. He stood up and took a peek at Jackson. He must be asleep.

It appeared that Jackson was using his jacket as a pillow case. I didn't know how heavy of a sleeper he was, but I thought it was unlikely that the guy could get it off of him without waking him. He'd also been smart enough to sleep with his shoes on. They would be gone by now if he hadn't. Jackson was sleeping on his stomach, which left his back pockets exposed. I really hoped that he had the sense to move his wallet.

In the next instant I learned two things. One, Jackson was a light sleeper. Two, he was not smart enough to move his wallet. The guy reached for his wallet but woke him in the process.

"Get away from me," came Jackson's muffled voice before the guy pulled him off of his bunk and threw him to the floor. He grabbed for Jackson's jacket and then threw a strong right hook to his jaw.

"Fuck," Jackson cursed and threw a punch of his own. He connected pretty hard with the guy's gut.

I was off my bunk in a heartbeat. Jackson getting robbed was one thing. Jackson getting his ass kicked was another.

I pulled the guy off and told them both to break it up. I got in a pretty good shot to the guy's head while I was at it, which was mildly satisfying. I hadn't been in a good street fight for a while.

The shelter workers interceded after that and proceeded to throw us all unceremoniously out into the rain. They didn't care if you fought, just so long as you didn't do it inside while everyone was sleeping.

Jackson had lost his jacket. The guy was running off down the street with it. I wasn't sure about his wallet.

I tried to slip off down the alley, but Jackson called to me before I could make my break. "Hey thanks," he said, "I'm not sure why you did that, but I appreciate it."

He had a bloody lip, but didn't look too bad all things considered. He was calmer than I thought he would be. His hands were shaking, but he wasn't running home.

I nodded my head at him and walked away. I was hoping he wouldn't follow me, or this whole gig would be up. He didn't. He turned and walked away. I let him get a few blocks before I doubled back to follow him. I called Sean to let him know that I needed him. I wouldn't do for Jackson to see me again tonight. We were going to have to change shifts early.

When Jackson Met Alissa

Jackson

Fuck. My jaw was killing me and my shoulder didn't feel too great either.

I ducked into a 24-hour McDonald's and managed to get into the men's room unnoticed.

I took a look in the mirror. It wasn't as bad as it could be. My lip was split and a little swollen. I needed ice, but even without it, I would heal. It really wasn't even that noticeable. My shoulder was bruised from where I had smacked it on the bed as the guy pulled me down from the top bunk, but it wasn't swollen, and I could rotate it.

I took a quick inventory. I still had my wallet, thank God, which meant that I had my birth certificate and remaining cash. I had lost my jacket though, which also meant that I had lost my soap, deodorant, and toothbrush. I ran some hot water in the sink and washed my face as best I could without hurting my lip. I was going to need to shave soon. My five o'clock shadow was turning into serious stubble. I could smell myself, too. *Lovely.*

I needed a better plan. There was no way I was going back

to that shelter tonight. I thought there was a chance that it would be dangerous, but now I realized that I stood out like a sore thumb among the homeless. I couldn't allow myself to be a target like that.

I wondered, and not for the first time, who that guy was that had helped me. I was grateful but confused. It was not in his best interest to jump in the middle of my fight, and I was sure that I would have been a lot worse off if he hadn't. I wished he would have stuck around for more than one reason. Having a friend in this world seemed like an invaluable asset. I wasn't liable to be that lucky twice.

I had actually gotten a fair amount of sleep, and I felt pretty well rested. That was good. I had a feeling that this would be a long day.

Maybe I should just give up on this whole ridiculous charade. I clearly was not cut out for this. I did have a stubborn streak a mile wide though, and part of me would never be content with letting Jason win.

If I was being completely honest with myself, I knew that it ran deeper than that. I wanted to prove to myself that my success in life was not just a hand-me-down from my parents. Yes, I had been born into money, but I had always believed that hard work had been the real key to my blessed life.

What if it wasn't? Could I really make it on my own without the support of my family? Of course, I could. That was stupid. Wasn't it?

One of the restaurant employees entered the restroom breaking me out of my musing. He shot me a dirty look and then closed himself in one of the stalls. I took that as my cue to leave. The only other occupants of the restaurant were two dark haired guys, both good sized, who were talking to each other and drinking coffee. They had their backs to me and didn't even glance my way as I wandered back out into the rain.

It was fucking cold. The rain pulled the heat right out of my skin and without my jacket I was going to be miserable until the sun came up. I needed somewhere to stay out of the rain, and I needed a game plan.

I headed back to the subway. It had been okay last night. My pass would be good until Friday, so at least I could stay mobile for a while. I sat in the back of the car again and looked out the window at nothing but miles of concrete tunneling. I was heading back to the area where the social security office was located.

I needed to come up with sixteen dollars to get that card. The kid at the shelter had politely told me to fuck off when I'd asked him to borrow the money. I had known that it would be a long shot. I wouldn't lend me money either. I wasn't going to beg though. I had said borrow and that was what I meant. I would have paid him back.

The good news was, I knew where to find lunch. I was hungrier than I had ever been in my life.

Daylight was once again beginning to filter into the subway stops so I exited about five blocks up from the social security office. I knew that there was no point to going in until I found a way to make the extra money that I needed, but I didn't have anywhere else to go.

I made an average of about thirty-five million dollars a year between buying and selling businesses, stocks, and other investments. That meant that I would have an hourly rate of a little less than $17,000 an hour if I worked a normal 40-hour workweek. How was it that I had suddenly become so incapable of earning $16 fucking dollars?

"Damn it, Matt," a female voice carried down the alley causing me to jerk my head up. The streets were very quiet this early in the morning, and with the rain, I was pretty much alone on the sidewalk. "I hired you, because I needed someone to show up on time. Don't bother coming in today, and if you're late tomorrow you're fired." She sounded pissed, but even angry, she had a beautiful voice.

I walked up the alley, in the direction of the voice. I stopped dead in my tracks when I spotted her. She was stunning. Long brown hair, slender build, perfect hips, and she was carrying what looked like a very heavy crate of live crabs. Their claws were taped shut, but one of the crabs had gotten partially free and its pinchers were opening and closing unnervingly close to her delicate fingers. She had a cell phone precariously perched on her shoulder, and she was practically screaming into it.

It took me a minute to understand the whole scene. She was halfway between a cargo van and the backdoor of what appeared to be a restaurant. She must have gone down to the docks to purchase fresh seafood for the restaurant. She was clearly trying to get the ingredients in through the door, and her help had obviously not shown up as she was screaming at him about being fired.

I watched in horror as the half-free crab slid sideways in the crate and pinched the side of her hand. She let out a shriek and dropped the crate. She tried to save it and instead somehow managed to tangle her feet together sending crabs flying as she fell to the ground. I sprinted out of the alley just a moment too late to catch her, but I did manage to keep the crate from falling on top of her.

I set it on the ground a few feet away and turned to help her get up. "Are you okay?" I asked.

Alissa

Oh God, how embarrassing.

My hand was bleeding from a stupid crab, my ass was in a mud puddle, and the hottest man that I had ever seen was asking me if I was okay.

No, I was not okay.

"Uh," I said stupidly. He was extending his hand to me and it took me a moment just to figure out why.

He's trying to help your stupid ass up.

"Yeah." I took a hold of his hand and tried not to behave

like a bumbling idiot. He managed to get me on my feet. His hand was freezing, but that was to be expected as he was out in the chilly morning rain with no coat.

"I'm Jackson," he said, pumping the hand that he was still holding in a very professional handshake.

"Alissa," I managed. He let go of my hand, and I was suddenly very disappointed with the loss of contact.

Get a hold of yourself!

Right. "Thanks, uh, for helping me up." I gave him a weak smile. I could feel my cheeks burning with my signature blush. How mortifying.

"No problem." He gave me a beautiful lopsided grin, and I literally thought that my heart had stopped for a moment. "Let me help you with these, uh, crabs."

Oh God. My crabs!

"Oh, shit," I said looking at the half-full crate. Several of my crab cake specials were trying to escape down the street. I caught up with them and somehow managed to get them all back in the box without hurting myself.

In accordance with my usual luck, it started to rain harder. We were both going to be drenched.

"Um, I really appreciate it, but you don't have to stand here getting soaked with me," I said.

Part of me really wished that he'd go away and put an end to my misery, and part of me really hoped that he would throw me down in the street for a little more mud wrestling.

"I have no where better to be," he replied, "and it sounds like you're a little short on help. Perhaps I can be of assistance?"

Oh, you can assist me any time.

"Yeah, Matt was late again today. He's supposed to be here to help me bring all the stuff in each morning, but he's kind of unreliable."

He picked up the crate and moved towards the door. "Where do you want them?" he asked.

"On the floor by the empty fish tank," I said. I pulled a box of vegetables from the van and followed him in. I ran my bloody hand under the tap. The bleeding had already stopped. Stupid crab.

With Jackson's help, I had the van unloaded and the fresh ingredients put away in record time.

My usual routine for the day was to wake up about 4:30 a.m., go down to the docks and the open-air market, buy my supplies for the day, bring the stuff in, go upstairs and take a shower in my apartment, and then come down and start cooking for the lunch crowd. I felt terrible about trying to throw Jackson out into the rain though, without any form of payment, wet muddy and smelling like crabs. I wanted to make it right.

"I feel so bad that you are all muddy because of me," I said. "I, uh, have an apartment above the restaurant here, with laundry. Why don't you come up and take a shower, and I'll throw your wet clothes in the dryer for you."

He looked at me with those beautiful blue eyes, and my brain completely shut off. *What was it about men with dark hair and blue eyes?*

"I mean," I stuttered, "if you're not in a hurry that is."

"Thank you, Alissa," *Oh God, he said my name.* "I would really appreciate that."

I stood there stupidly.

Right. Upstairs.

I pulled the kitchen door shut and then led the gorgeous man up the steps to my tiny apartment. I had opened my restaurant less than a year ago, and every penny I had was poured into it. I was doing quite well, actually, for being a young small business owner, but between working so many hours and needing to buy so much for the restaurant, I hadn't found the time nor the money to really furnish my apartment.

It was sparse, but it was home.

"Uh, the bathroom is right here," I said, flipping on the light. "Just wait one second, and I will get you a towel and something to change into."

I didn't really have any guy's clothes lying around my apartment, but I found an oversized t-shirt and a pair of boxer shorts that I sometimes slept in, and I thought they would work well enough until his clothes dried.

"I'm gonna' go start breakfast, but just put your wet clothes out here in the hall, and I'll put them in to dry for you."

"You are too kind," he said. "Thank you for this."

"I should be thanking you," I said. "You're the one who's done all the work."

He smiled at me again and then gently shut the bathroom door. I went out to the kitchen to start breakfast. Usually, I just made oatmeal, but I had behaved like an incompetent fool all morning, and I was desperate to show the beautiful boy in my bathroom that I could do something right. I was going to make my signature breakfast - stuffed French toast.

I heard the bathroom door open and close, so I went to collect his wet things for the dryer. Whew! His clothes stunk. How odd. I mean I knew we were working up a sweat bringing in the food, and the rain always made it worse, but either he was out for a jog in the rain in his jeans or he'd been in these clothes a while. I was guessing it was the latter. I had intended to just dry his clothes, but these really needed to be washed, so I tossed them into my washer along with a couple of dirty towels.

What a strange man. His jeans were an incredibly expensive brand. So expensive, in fact, that I wouldn't even know what they were if it weren't for Lexy. She was my best friend of fifteen years, and she made a living as a personal assistant and professional shopper. She was constantly trying to educate me in the ways of the rich and famous. Most of what she said passed right through my brain, but occasionally something would stick.

What was a man, who could afford these jeans, doing out in the rain at 5:30 on a Thursday morning with no jacket? And better yet, why did his clothes smell like a homeless shelter?

I changed my clothes and pulled my hair up out of my face, and then went back to the kitchen. I cracked a couple of eggs into a bowl while I pondered. By the time the water shut off in the shower, I had the strawberries cut, coffee made, orange juice squeezed, and toast in the frying pan. Jackson appeared a few minutes later, looking much fresher and even more amazing than before. I hadn't noticed it, but his brown hair had these wonderful highlights in it.

I let my eyes travel over his face. Oh God, he had a split lip. How had I not seen that? Was he in a fight?

"Something smells fantastic," he said, and his stomach rumbled in agreement.

I laughed. "I'm glad you came hungry."

I put four thick slices of French toast on a plate for him and told him to sit down. "Did you want coffee or orange juice?"

"Both please, if you don't mind."

"I don't mind at all." I fixed my own breakfast and then sat down next to him at my tiny kitchen table. "So tell me, how is that you happened to be in the alley behind my restaurant so early this morning?" I was being nosy, I know, but I had to have some answers.

"Um, I was… I was walking down the main street out here, and I heard you scream into your phone, and I thought you might be in trouble, so I came to investigate."

"Oh. Well, that was very nice of you," I said, but I had a feeling that he knew that was not the answer I was looking for. "Why were you walking down the street?"

He was eating incredibly fast. He was almost done with his plate, and I'd barely gotten a bite of mine. I got up and added two more slices to the pan. It looked like he could eat them. When he saw what I was doing he smiled gratefully.

"I was in search of breakfast actually," he said, gesturing to his plate. "And this is the most incredible French toast I have ever eaten. Is all your food this good?"

His answer made absolutely no sense, and I was quite sure that he knew it, which is why he was trying to distract me with compliments on my food.

"Most people like it," I said. I wasn't letting him off the hook that easy though. "Are you from out of town or something?"

"Uh, no. I'm just kind of in transition right now, and I'm keeping some odd hours." He was a master at not actually giving me any information.

He cleaned his plate quite easily and managed to get through the rest of our breakfast conversation with me still completely clueless as to who or what he was. I was beginning to think that he was really a superhero in disguise. It would explain the odd hours, the smelly designer clothes, the appetite, and his ability to keep that crate of crabs from crushing me.

"Thank you so very much for breakfast, Alissa," he said, "but I'm sure I'm keeping you from something."

"Oh, well you can't go yet," I said. "I put your clothes in the wash, so let me just throw them in the dryer. They are going to need about forty-five minutes to dry. Unfortunately, I do need to get started on the lunch prep. My other employees, who are thankfully more reliable than Matt, should be arriving soon."

I put his clothes in the dryer. "You can come down to the kitchen if you want, or you're welcome to hang out up here and watch TV or whatever until they are dry."

"I'd like to stay with you," he said.

Forever. I thought. You can stay with me forever.

Who am I?

Jackson

Her French toast was incredible. She was incredible. And she was going to think that I was completely insane. There was no possible way that I could explain this to her.

Yeah, I'm a really rich and successful guy, who just got his ass kicked in a homeless shelter, and I helped you carry all that stuff in here because I think you're beautiful and because I'm hoping that you'll give me $16 so I can work tonight and win a bet against my brother. Oh, and thanks for the shower, by the way. It was great, but I'm going to be sporting a hard-on for the rest of day because the shampoo that I used smells like you and it's the most incredible thing I've ever smelled – well second only to your French toast, of course.

I was so fucked.

One of the problems with having money was that you never knew if the girls were after you or your cash. Truthfully, it had never mattered that much to me either way. I had no interest in most women, other than a natural physical attraction; I found them to be shallow. Alissa was no ordinary woman. She wore no makeup, and her clothes were not expensive, but she was all the more beautiful for it. She made it look effortless. She struck me as a really genuine person. There was nothing fake about this girl.

When this week was over, I was going to eat here, in her restaurant, every damn day.

After breakfast, I followed her downstairs so she could start her work. I was still wearing her clothes which were too tight and probably looked ridiculous, and I was barefoot, but I didn't feel the least bit awkward. I had a feeling that I would always be comfortable in her presence.

I decided to drill her with as many questions as possible. I wanted to know everything about her. And, if we kept the conversation about her, I could keep the spotlight off of myself.

"So how long have you owned this restaurant?"

"Just under a year I guess," she said.

"What made you open it?"

She went on to tell me how it had been her childhood dream to be this great professional chef, and she spoke about it with such passion that I became truly envious. I liked my job, and I was good at it, but I didn't have a tenth of the passion that she did when it came to my work. This place was her life.

I sat on a stool in the corner and watched in amazement as she handled the live crabs with practiced skill. Her hands quickly and efficiently moved steaming pots, juggled sharp knives, and avoided danger after danger. All of the clumsy fumbling that I had witnessed earlier was banished from her kitchen. In here, she was a force to be reckoned with.

I asked about her family, her hobbies, her favorite color, food, flowers, everything I could think of until she finally told me that I wasn't allowed to ask any more questions and sent me upstairs to check on the clothes in the dryer. I was reluctant to leave her, but I was reminded of reality. I needed to get that social security card today.

Several of her employees had arrived while I was

captivated by the sound of her voice, and her kitchen was now bustling with activity. I paused in the stairwell to watch her interact with the others. Her easy conversation and playful teasing were punctuated with instructions to her crew. She would be a wonderful boss, although I was sure she was too nice. It would probably break her heart to fire someone – that Matt she was on the phone with this morning for example. I would have fired his ass the first time he didn't show up. I had never shown mercy in the corporate world. I was not cruel, but I did have very high standards. People who disappointed me were not around very long. It was just business, but here, in her kitchen, it didn't feel like business. It felt like family.

My clothes were dry so I changed back into them, folded the towels that she had also dried, and left the clothes that she had lent me on her bed.

I took the opportunity to snoop around her bedroom while I was here alone. She had a couple of photos. I assumed the man in the police uniform was her father – she'd said he was a police chief in small town not far from here. *Please don't shoot me, sir, but I am extremely attracted to your daughter.*

I contemplated that for a few minutes. I wanted to meet him, everyone, everyone who had ever been close to Alissa. I was shocked to discover that I was considering a real relationship with this woman. I'd only known her for a couple of hours, but I was already helpless in her presence.

So what the hell was I doing? I was pretending to be someone I wasn't. Of course, she didn't have any idea who I was. I had seen to that, but I knew I wouldn't get away with avoiding her questions forever, and truthfully I didn't want to. I wanted her to know who I was. The real me -- not the billionaire businessman that society thought I was, not the homeless man I was pretending to be -- just the Jackson that got to sit barefoot in Alissa's kitchen.

I made my way back downstairs in time to catch the end of her conversation. I was eavesdropping, and I knew it was wrong, but I was desperate for as much information as I could possibly get about this woman.

"Ty, it is none of your damn business who he is," she said.

"I'm just looking out for you, 'Lissa. I mean, sure, you can sleep with whomever you want, but he was sitting in your kitchen, in your clothes, and he didn't even know what your favorite food was. Every other person in this room can answer that question. I never thought of you as the type to sleep around, but you don't know that guy at all."

"I'm not sleeping with him, you asshole. He helped me, and he got muddy in the process. I let him use my shower, and that's it. That's also the end of this discussion. And if you ever imply that I am easy again, I will so fire your ass. I don't care if you are the best dessert man I've got working for me."

I came around the corner in enough time to watch her hurl an empty crab shell at him. She missed by a mile, but it was still adorable.

"Yeah, because you make that signature French toast of yours for every random person who uses your shower," he smirked at her. "And for the record, I'm the only dessert man you've got working for you."

So that *was* a special breakfast that she made for me. My heart was delighted by that news. I cleared my throat to alert them to my presence and shot Tyler a dirty look. I was grateful to him for inadvertently letting me know about the French toast, but I was pissed at him for implying that Alissa was anything less than a lady, even if it was meant to be playful. She hadn't taken offense, but she still deserved better.

"Thank you, Alissa," I said, "for a delightful morning, but I should be on my way now." She looked as disappointed as I felt. "I'd like to see you again sometime, if that would be okay with you?"

The smile that lit up her face warmed my heart, and it took every ounce of willpower that I had to not pull her into my arms. "I'd like that," she said quietly. The beautiful blush was back on her cheeks.

I wanted to leave her my number, but I didn't have my phone. At least I knew where she lived, and worked, for that matter. It wouldn't be hard to find her again. I started for the door.

"Wait! Let me pay you for your work this morning."

"Oh, I couldn't possibly," the standard refusal fell from my lips before I even thought about it. I needed the money, but I really didn't want to take it from her. I also didn't want her to see me as an employee.

"I insist," she said. She ducked into a closet for a moment and returned with a $20 bill in her hand. "It's the least I can do."

I mumbled a thank you, and reluctantly took the bill from her. She walked me to the backdoor.

"Have a wonderful day, my beautiful Alissa." I lifted her hand and placed a kiss just above her knuckles, hoping to dispel any further thoughts of me as the hired help, and then I walked into the alley and away from the most amazing creature I'd ever met.

Running the World

Jason

Why did Jackson have to be such a morning person? I was at the office a full hour earlier than I had ever been here in my life. When we made this stupid bet, I had not planned on doing Jackson's job in addition to my own, but as soon as Shelby found out, everything changed. She personally saw to it that this week would be a living hell for me.

I wouldn't have told her about the bet at all, but she overheard the second half of my phone call with Ben on the night that we made the bet, and she freaked out on me as soon as I hung up.

"Where exactly is Jackson?" she asked.

"Uh, well..." I scrambled for an excuse.

"You sent him out into the city alone with no keys and no money at midnight so that he could pretend to be homeless? Are you insane? Exactly how fucking drunk were you?"

She'd gone on like that for a full fifteen minutes, not allowing me to interrupt. When she finally ceased her ranting, she schooled me on how this week was going to go in lieu of Jackson's disappearing act. She made it clear that I would handle all of Jackson's responsibilities at work. If I failed in any way, I would not be sleeping in the same bed as my own wife... for a month.

Fucking cock-blocking brother. How had I let him get me into this?

I pinched the bridge of my nose. Oh no! I was picking up Jackson's mannerisms now, too. No wonder that boy is always so stressed out; no one should work this many hours or start this early in the morning. I should still be at home in bed with my smokin' hot wife.

Jackson and I worked together in the "family business." Jackson filled the CEO position and managed the major acquisitions. For all intents and purposes, he ran the company. I was also on the board, which meant that I assisted in the major decisions, but my main day-to-day duty was serving as the primary Hayes representative to the press. My whole job was to be "likeable," and I was damn good at it. Jackson intimidated people. I made sure that we still had a favorable image in the community.

I'd spent most of the day yesterday listening to reports from Jackson's various employees regarding the productivity of companies we had recently purchased, current status of companies we were purchasing, and feasibility for companies that we might purchase in the future. I thought that my head was going to explode. I hadn't made one real decision all day, and I was already exhausted.

It seemed that Jackson was making a better homeless person than I was making a CEO. His brain must be going a million different directions all the time. No wonder he'd never managed to fit a woman into his life. His mental capacity had to be maxed out.

I jumped when my phone rang unexpectedly. Ben was supposed to call me every afternoon with an update, so just one glance at the caller ID was enough to scare the shit out of me. He was calling at 7:00 in the morning. That meant that something had happened to Jackson.

"Ben, what's wrong? What happened?"

"Calm down, Jason. He's okay."

"Then why are you calling and giving me a heart attack?"

"Jackson got in a little fight last night in the shelter. He's fine. He's just got a split lip and the guy managed to take off with his jacket. I punched the guy pretty hard in the head, but everyone lived to tell the tale. I don't think Jackson's onto me. Sean's got him now."

Oh God. He was in a fight. I had to put a stop to this. It could have been so much worse. It wasn't worth the risk. What were we thinking?

"Ben, I want you to tell him to call it off."

"Sean? I can't tell Sean to leave him. We might lose him."

"No. I mean I want to tell Jackson to stop it. This is too damn dangerous. Where is he? I'm going to talk to him."

"He's fine. Don't overreact. He's tougher than I thought. He took that punch like a man."

I did not want to hear about my brother taking punches like a man. Whoever hit him had better pray that I never found out who they were or the smack to the head that he'd gotten from Ben would seem like child's play.

"I want to know where he is, Ben." I was practically growling at him.

"I don't know man. I left him with Sean. They were on the subway. They could be anywhere.

"Shit. Well, you can get a hold of Sean right? I am going into the office. I have to cover this stupid ass meeting and then I am going to pick Jackson up. I'll call you as soon as I am done, and I'll expect you to know where he is."

"Jason, really, he's fine, but if that's the way you want it, I'll tell you where he is when you call back."

"Thank you." I closed the phone.

If it was any other meeting I would blow it off, but this was for the Nick Carver buyout that Jackson had been so freaked out over. Nick had called late yesterday and demanded an early meeting. I'd had very little prep time. If Jackson had known about it, he probably would have dropped the whole homeless charade and handled it himself. I didn't know what Nick wanted, but I had a feeling that Jackson's leaving and his sudden desire to talk to me were not mutually exclusive events. He wanted to capitalize on Jackson's absence.

I didn't have time to get Jackson and bring him to the meeting, and truthfully I didn't trust the board to make the right decisions without us. Nick was a manipulative bastard, and I couldn't leave him alone with my staff. There were just too many ways that he could cause trouble. His company might be a good investment, but Jackson was right to be leery of him.

When I arrived at the office, I was surprised to find that I was alone in the conference room. Had they moved the meeting and not told me? I couldn't even complete the thought before Nick walked through the door.

"Mr. Hayes." His voice was cold.

"Mr. Carver, you'll have to forgive me, I am not sure where the rest of the board is at the present time..." He cut me off.

"I told them that this meeting was canceled," he said. "I was hoping to speak to you alone."

"You could have simply requested a private meeting, Mr. Carver, although I have nothing to say to you that I would not say in front of the board."

"I received word that your brother was vacationing in Hawaii. Unfortunate timing, don't you think? I am concerned that perhaps he isn't as dedicated to your company as you may believe."

I drew myself up to my full intimidating height. *What exactly was he implying?*

"Jackson's dedication is not in question here. He is very loyal to this company, and I do not appreciate your suggestion to the contrary."

"Really, Mr. Hayes? Are you aware that Jackson has tried, on multiple occasions, to convince your board not to buy my company?"

"Yes, I am." *He doesn't like you, because you're a sneaky rat bastard.*

"Are you aware that he made me a second offer for my company?"

I was not aware of that. Why would he do that?

"He came to me personally, at my office, and attempted to buy me out with his own personal assets. He wanted to beat you to the punch and keep the financial gain for himself."

"Jackson would never do that."

This asshole was really starting to piss me off.

"Oh, I assure you he did - smart man really. Why should he settle for less than thirty percent when he can afford to buy me out himself and keep all of it?" The jerk had the nerve to smirk at me. "Makes me wonder what else he has stolen from this company right under your nose, Mr. Hayes."

"My brother is an honest man," I said, "and if that's all that you came here for, you can leave now. We're finished."

"Surely, Mr. Hayes, you don't believe that I would make these kinds of accusations without proof." He produced a manila envelope. "I believe you'll want to make some adjustments after you've reviewed this. I'll be expecting your call."

With that, he turned and walked out of my conference room, leaving me alone with his mysterious envelope. I simply stared at it for a while, unsure of what to do. Part of me was curious, of course, but most of me knew it was bullshit. Jackson would never go behind my back on something like this. I was not dumb enough to take Nick's word for it. I was sure that the envelope contained forged documents. He probably got a hold of Jackson's signature and thought that a couple of signed, photocopied documents would be enough to set me against my own brother.

I opened the envelope and dumped the contents onto the table. It did in fact contain documents, like I had expected. I was about the throw the whole thing in the trash when I noticed a silver disc in the pile. An audio CD? Really?

My own morbid curiosity got the better of me. I carried it to my office and pushed the disc into my computer. Jackson's voice filled my ears.

Oh God. He taped the conversation.

I was listening to Jackson's sales pitch as he tried to buy the company behind my back.

"Personal assets… without involving Hayes Industries…"

I couldn't listen any more. How could this be true? My own brother.

I flipped open my phone.

"Ben, where the hell is he?"

Thicker than Water

Jackson

I felt like my head was in a fog that I just couldn't shake. I really wanted to focus on getting my social security card, but my every thought involved Alissa. I just couldn't get that woman out of my mind: the way she smelled, the way she smiled, the way she wouldn't take any shit from her employees. God, I was pathetic. I felt like I could just float around this city all day and be happy. She was incredible.

Out of nowhere, strong arms grabbed me by the front of my shirt. My back was slammed up against a brick wall. The air rushed from my lungs. My head snapped up to face my attacker.

"Jason! What the fuck?!" I screamed, my heart rate lowering when I saw it was just my brother. "You scared the shit out of me."

Where was the playful smile that I was expecting? He wasn't letting go of my shirt.

"What's wrong?"

"How could you?" he growled at me.

"How could I what?" I asked. My mind was reeling. Did this have something to do with Alissa? All I'd done was hang out with her all morning. What could possibly make him this angry?

"Don't play dumb with me, Jackson. How could you go behind my back and try to buy the Carver Company yourself? All that bullshit about not trusting Nick, while it was you who was being a deceptive little shit?"

"Fuck Jason, did he tell you that? You believe that I would lie to you for financial gain? Have you lost your fucking mind? Put me down, you gorilla, and we'll talk about this." His hands didn't loosen on my shirt. God, he was really pissed.

Fucking Nick. I hated that bastard. This had probably been his idea all along, to drive a wedge between brothers so that our company would fail.

"No, he didn't tell me that. He gave me a goddamn recording of the conversation. I have your fucking voice on tape, telling him that you want to buy his company without involving our business. That's fucking evidence, Jackson."

Shit. Nick had recorded our conversation and was trying to make it look like I wanted to keep the profits for myself. "Fuck man, I swear to God I can explain, but you're seriously hurting me. Get a hold of yourself."

"Tell me," he said, pushing me further into the wall. "Tell me how the fuck he got that recording."

"Jason, you know I don't want to buy that company. I have always thought this was a bad deal. I don't care how many times the reports come back clean, Nick is a lying, deceitful sack of shit, and there is something crooked in that business. I just haven't found it yet. I went to his office and offered to buy him out personally because I don't want his company to be a liability to our company."

He still had me in a death grip, but I could see that my words were starting to sink in.

"You and the rest of the board wouldn't listen to me when

I said that this whole thing was a bad idea. You know that my vote alone can't override a majority decision. So I offered him more money, my personal assets, because I wanted to protect the company that you and I have worked so damn hard to build together. If I owned it personally, and it went bad, I would have simply buried it and taken the financial loss myself. If I was wrong, and the company was a success, I could have merged it into our joint business any time. I would never fucking steal from you, Jason. Never.

I'm telling you, that man is a crook. He wouldn't accept my offer, which makes me even more suspicious of him. He should have sold the business to the highest bidder, but he didn't, which means that he wants Hayes Enterprises specifically to buy him out. He has to have a reason for that, and now, from what you've told me, I'm guessing that driving a wedge between us is a big part of that plan."

His eyes widened, and he took a step back. It was like something had finally clicked in his brain, and he was processing the fact that he had his brother pinned against a brick wall in an alley. His hands relaxed.

"Oh God, Jackson. I'm sorry; are you okay?" He was in some odd emotional state between rage and horror, and if I wasn't terrified, it might have been funny. I would not ever want to be on Jason's bad side.

I nodded that I was. I bent over with my hands on my knees trying to return my breathing to a normal speed.

"Fuck man. I thought you were going to kill me." A nervous laugh escaped my lips. "All that over a business transaction? Remind me never to screw you over. Seriously." I could see that he was returning to his usual senses.

"You're that sure that this is a bad idea?" he asked. "You really would have bought him out just so that you could take the risk on yourself?"

"Yes, Jason," I said. "I'm sorry I didn't discuss it further with you before I went to him, but you were backing the board's decision, and I thought you had your mind made up.

I was pretty sure that he wouldn't sell to me anyway, and I didn't want to drag you any further into this mess."

"Well shit," he said, finally laughing like the brother I was used to. "Next time just come tell me that we're not fucking buying the business, and I'll vote with you. If you really feel that strongly about it, I won't go against you. You're not usually wrong, and even if you are, I'd rather be wrong with you than right with a man like Nick Carver. I knew you didn't like him, but I had no idea you were that serious about it."

"He's up to no good, Jason. I can't prove it, but I know it in my very bones. We should not be buying that company."

"Fine man, we'll go call a meeting with the board right now. I'll change my vote, and we'll cancel the deal." He looked at me then and laughed. "Well, maybe we should get you back in a suit first, and you need to shave. You're scruffy as shit, brother. How's the jaw feel? Ben said you got hit pretty hard."

My head snapped up. "Who's Ben?"

Jason

Fuck. I was doing a lot of screwing up today. Jackson had just told me that he was trying to protect my stupid ass from financial ruin and then I go and blurt out that I've been trying to protect his stupid ass from physical ruin. We were a matched pair weren't we?

"Ben's the bodyguard that I hired to protect you while you were doing this homeless thing," I admitted. "He's the one that jumped on the guy in the shelter. He's been following you around since Tuesday night."

I was afraid he'd be pissed, but he was doubled over in laughter.

"I wondered why the fuck some homeless guy would jump in on my fight. You hired a fucking bodyguard to watch me be homeless for a week? That shit is too funny." He was gasping for breath and there were tears running down his cheeks. "And here I thought I was doing it all on my own. I was actually kind of proud of myself. I should have known I couldn't do it."

He was getting his laughter under control, but there was a hint of disappointment in his eyes. He must have been taking this man versus world struggle more seriously than I thought.

"Speaking of which, we're going to start eating three meals a day at this restaurant that I found. Well, two meals a day, because I don't think she's open for breakfast, but she should be because she makes the best French toast in the world."

Being homeless had clearly gone to his head. "What on earth are you rambling on about?" I asked, totally confused.

"Alissa," he said, as if that explained everything. "She makes amazing French toast."

The New Plan

Jackson

So Jason and I decided that we needed to sit and talk for a while. Obviously, we were going to have to come up with a new plan. We needed to call a board meeting, but I wanted to have the whole thing worked out ahead of time. If Jason and I both voted "no" to buying the Carver Company, then we would no longer have a majority and the negotiations would end immediately. Together, we controlled sixty percent of the vote. When we were in agreement, we could pretty much run the company however we wanted.

There were four other board members, Robert, Kayla, Nithin, and Kristin, who were also investors in the company. We could run the company without them, but we'd learned that it was better to have people on the board who had a vested interest in the business. It was also good to have a second opinion, or in this case four opinions. They brought diversity to the table, and we were stronger for it.

The Carver deal had come to us originally through Robert. He saw Nick as an up-and-coming powerhouse, so he'd monitored his businesses for the last three years or so.

When he felt that Nick had acquired enough experience to be noteworthy, we'd assigned Kayla the task of beginning the official due diligence to decide whether to make the acquisition.

Jason and I settled into a coffee shop where we could speak uninterrupted and begin our planning. The way I saw it, we had two options. One, call a meeting immediately and stop the deal or two, pretend for a while that we were still going to move forward. If we did the latter, Jason could perhaps flush out Nick's true motives. Either way, I felt a million times better now that I had Jason on my side. It meant a lot to me that he was willing to take my word for it.

"So, here's what I was thinking," Jason said. "We should hold off on making any official decisions for now. Let the board continue to think that you're in Hawaii. I'll call Nick, and you can listen in on speaker. I can pretend that I'm still mad at you, and hopefully, I can get him to tell me what he really wants. We can make a decision based on what he says."

"I think that's smart. I am worried about both Bob and Kayla. We know she's always been pushy, but they were both really adamant about buying this company. It doesn't sit well with me. I think it would be best if we kept all of this information between us for now."

"Agreed. So what are we going to do about you?" He laughed.

"What about me?" I asked.

"Well, we're going to have to hide you, since you're supposed to be on vacation. What do you want to do for the rest of the week?"

"I don't really know. To be honest, our whole bet slipped my mind when you started talking about Nick Carver, but this has been quite an experience for me. I'm not sure that I'm ready to give up being homeless yet."

"You can't be serious. You got punched by a thief in the

middle of the night, for crying out loud!"

"Yeah, I know, man," I said, "but there have been some really great parts, too. I was kind of looking forward to learning to tend bar. You know? It's an experience that I've never had, and I'll probably suck at it, but I'd like to try. For once in my life, Jason, I feel like I'm really making it on my own steam. Our parents are awesome people, but you know that they handed everything to us. For once, I want to feel like I earned it from the ground up."

"Jackson, you work very hard. I spent one damn day doing your job, and I was exhausted. You shouldn't feel like you haven't earned your life."

"I know. I don't mean it like that. I just mean that when I look at self-made people, like Alissa, I think they have so much to be proud of. Maintaining a business is hard work, but what's another million dollars on a business that was already making millions? Honestly, it's more of a challenge trying to get a social security card in this town."

"So that's what this is really about?" Jason said with a wide smile.

"What's that?"

"A girl! You want to stay homeless because you want to be with this girl." His signature boisterous laugh filled the room. "I never thought I'd see the day."

Jason

When I left Jackson and headed back to the office, I felt like a thousand pounds had been lifted off of my shoulders. I could be such an idiot sometimes. I was still kicking myself for ever having doubted my own brother. He might have a stick up his ass, but I knew better than to think he would ever screw me over, especially over a company that might be worth fifteen million dollars a year at most. Jackson already had a ton of money - we both did - and I should have known that money no longer motivated him. We both worked for a variety of reasons: we wanted our parents to be proud of us, we wanted to be proud of ourselves, and we enjoyed our jobs. The money didn't really matter anymore, but Nick didn't understand that, and I had forgotten it for a brief time.

As weird as it was, I understood why he wanted to do this homeless thing. Of course, it wasn't at all like being a real homeless person. Homeless people didn't have social graces embedded in them from an early age; they couldn't charm their way into jobs. They didn't have college educations. Most homeless people were also battling mental illness, illiteracy, a history of abuse, and a whole host of other things. Jackson still had an unfair advantage, but for him, this was a big step. I only hoped that he might learn to relax a little. He was so damn serious all the time, and I thought this experience might just teach him to not sweat the small stuff.

So, I'd made him promise to stay in a cheap hotel instead of a shelter, and I'd called off Ben and Sean. We put them to work following Nick instead. I was hoping that they might dig up some information that would be helpful to us.

I gave Jackson back one of his credit cards in case he really needed something. I gave him back his cell phone as well, but he was bound and determined to only use it if it was really necessary. He really wanted to try to finish this week out under his own power. I'd agreed, but we were going to meet every day for lunch just so I could check on him, and so we could continue to talk about Nick. I was going to have my secretary schedule a call for tomorrow that Jackson would be monitoring.

I'd prodded for information about this mysterious Alissa before I left, but after a few basic facts he'd gone shy on me and simply promised to let me meet her in the near future. I was fucking delighted. She sounded like the perfect fit for him, and truthfully, I was glad that she'd met him under false pretenses, or no pretenses at all. Women were funny around Jackson. They were attracted to his money and they were attracted to his good looks, but I didn't think that there had ever been a woman who lasted long enough to actually be attracted to Jackson. He had incredibly high standards, and he intimidated the shit out of most people.

I really hoped this would work out for him, and I really hoped we would manage to nail Nick with something, too. No one came between my brother and me without consequences.

A New Trade

Jackson

Wow. What a day. I was punched in the jaw by a homeless man. I saved a beautiful woman from a crate full of crabs. I had an amazing breakfast with the aforementioned damsel in distress. I was attacked by my own brother, who then accused me of corporate theft, before plotting, with the same brother to take down the real crooks. It wasn't even noon!

I had been on my way to the social security office when Jason accosted me, and I would need to head back there now. I was pretending to not have a limitless credit card or my iPhone. I really was proud of my efforts so far, and I was going to finish this week out if it killed me. A bet's a bet, corporate espionage aside.

One boring wait later, I was the proud owner of a new social security card or a temporary one anyway. The real copy wouldn't come in the mail for another thirty days.

I was hungry again, but also once again out of money, and what I really wanted to do was take a nap. It had been one hell of a day. I thought back to the park that was across the street from the bar. It seemed like forever ago that I had sat there waiting for the grill to open so that I could apply for a job. It wasn't a bad place to sit, and I thought it might be a decent place for a nap as well. I curled up on the park bench and closed my eyes.

When I woke, the light was different in the park. I had slept longer than I thought I would. My body was not accustomed to these odd hours.

I sat up and brushed an old wrapper from a fast food burger off of my legs. I stared at the crumpled paper for a moment in disbelief. I picked it up and turned it over in my hands. It seemed like an odd coincidence that the wind had carried it onto my sleeping form. There were no overfull trash cans for it to have blown out of. It was almost like it had been thrown. Was it possible that someone would deliberately put trash on another person while they slept? Having never slept on a park bench before, I wasn't entirely sure. I found a proper trash can and disposed of the paper resolving to push it from my mind.

I still had a half an hour until my shift, so I went to a Wendy's a few blocks up to use the men's room. I felt surprisingly rested, and I was looking forward to my first shift as a bartender.

"Romeo returns," Buddy said, when I walked through the door. "Welcome to your first official day." He threw me a T-shirt with the name of the bar across the back. "Put that on. I'll expect you to wear it every time you work."

"Yes, sir," I smiled. Not only did I get a job, but it came with free clothes!

"Cut that 'sir' shit out," he said. "Tonight you are working with Jessica." He pointed to the young blond behind the bar. "She'll help you get started. Jessica, meet Jackson."

She looked up from behind the bar and flashed me a smile. I knew that smile. I had seen it on hundreds of women before, right before they threw themselves at me. *I wonder if I can convince her that I'm gay?* It was going to be a long night.

"Jessica," I said politely, "it's a pleasure to meet you."

"You, too," she said, and then she giggled. *God, what an awful laugh.* "So, Jackson," she purred as she leaned forward on the bar, showing off far more cleavage than I really had a desire to see, "it's your first night?"

Really? What tipped you off?

"Yeah," I said lamely.

"Great, we are going to have so much fun!" She laughed again, but then, thankfully made herself useful by showing me where everything was. The place was moderately crowded. A few people were sitting at the bar, drinking after work, and a few were at the tables finishing up late dinners. Jessica was also acting as a waitress tonight, so she left frequently to check on her tables while I manned the bar. So far, I thought I was doing pretty well, but it was mostly requests for beer. I hadn't gotten any difficult drinks.

Truthfully, it was kind of boring. I don't know what I expected at 10:00 on a Thursday night but I had hoped for a better crowd and better tips. About 10:15 a man and a woman sat at the bar and requested menus, so I got to take my first food order. Jessica showed me how to enter it in the computer and how to get the food when it was ready. That was good; food orders meant bigger tips.

By midnight I'd made less than $40 and was ready to quit this shitty job. Jessica was grating on my very last nerve, Buddy hadn't re-appeared all night, and there was no way that anyone could live on this kind of a salary.

That's when my saving grace walked in the door. A group of five giggling girls in halter tops and short skirts, which were really quite inappropriate for the weather, sat down at the bar. They announced that it was the blond in the middle's twenty-first birthday, and they'd come out at midnight so that she could exercise her new right to drink. I carded them, gave them my best smile, and prepared to make a killing.

I have never worked so hard in my life. I made Flaming

Dr. Peppers, Hot Caramel Apples, Red Headed Sluts, and even a Blow Job for the birthday girl. I took pictures of them with their cameras, I posed with them in pictures, and I learned how to use a blender.

A group of guys about the same age joined them around 12:30, and I suddenly had a whole new set of shots and drinks to learn. These were easier and more expensive. About half way through the second set of Irish Car Bombs I wondered what else I had neglected to learn in college. I had a great time, and so did they.

The whole party stumbled out of the bar just before 2 a.m., and I started my clean-up. I was starving, exhausted, and I smelled like a bar, but I had earned every damn penny of the $152 I made. Buddy showed up to take my register and count it while I was cleaning up. Jessica gave him a positive progress report on me, and he smirked at me knowingly.

I left around 2:30 and set off to find a 24-hour diner or pizza place. I wanted the greasiest food I could find. Tom's Diner didn't disappoint. I had a burger and onion rings that I knew I would regret later. I absolutely devoured them. I followed it up with apple pie and coffee. The food perked me up, and I found that I wasn't tired. In fact, I was positively giddy. I was proud of my honest day's labor, and I felt like I had experienced a whole new world. I wanted to share it with someone.

Alissa. Just thinking about her made me suddenly very lonely. My stomach turned at the thought of spending the rest of the night in a cold hotel room. I wondered what it would be like to watch her sleeping, her beautiful brown hair fanned out on her pillow. I wondered what she slept in. Oh, God, I was going to embarrass myself if I thought any further along that line, so instead I paid my check and stepped out into the cold night air. It was already almost four in the morning. I wondered what time Alissa left for the market.

There was only one way to find out.

Alissa

The alarm went off at 4:30 like usual, and I smacked it with the palm of my hand. It was a good thing that I loved my job or I would never get up like this. I pulled on jeans and a t-shirt with my black hoodie over top. I had sneakers that were specifically for the market. After the fifth time I stepped in a pile of fish guts down there, I decided to designate a pair of fish-gut shoes.

I put my hair up in a ponytail and grabbed my wallet. I checked to make sure that I had enough cash for the day's groceries and my list. I always bought whatever looked good for the day, but there were staples that I needed to pick up as well.

I wondered if Matt would show up today. I hated to fire him, but he was irresponsible. I'd given him the job in the first place as a favor to his father. The Ozwell family owned a chain of sporting goods stores, and I had worked at one of them for a couple of years while I was putting myself through college. The Ozwells had been very good to me, so I didn't hesitate to employ their son. Matt was a college kid, just picking up a couple hours of work every day for spending money. Unfortunately, he also liked to party, which meant that he was rarely up by six when I needed him.

Of course, I was glad he hadn't shown up yesterday, because I wouldn't have met Jackson otherwise.

Jackson. My fancy-jeans-wearing, messy-haired, blue-eyed, superhero. *Swoon.*

I was such a girl. I mean seriously, who thinks like that?

I stumbled down the steps and out the backdoor with my keys in one hand and my list in the other.

"Good morning, Beautiful."

"Ack!!!" I screamed, and jumped a good three feet in the air. On the way down, I somehow twisted my feet beneath me, and I would have landed flat on my ass had I not been caught by a strong pair of arms.

Yep. Definitely a superhero.

"Oh no. I'm so sorry. I didn't mean to scare you," he apologized profusely.

"You scared the fuck out of me, Jackson," I said, finally righting myself and punching him in the bicep. "Don't ever do that again."

"I'm so sorry. I didn't expect you to react like that. I mean, of course, I won't do that again…" He was actually really cute when he was rambling. I decided to save him.

"I was just surprised to see you. What are you doing here?" Half of my brain was screaming, "He's a psycho killer here to stalk you!" The other half was insisting that I was glad he'd missed me. I knew I'd missed him.

"Well, I just got off work, and I was passing by, and I thought that perhaps you might like some company for your morning trip to the market. I'm sorry. I should have called, but I didn't get your number, and…" He ran his hand through his already disheveled hair. "Well… the truth is, I just wanted to see you."

He turned those beautiful eyes on me like a puppy that knew it was about to be chastised and gave me a sheepish grin. I was done for.

"I would love to have your company for my trip to the market," I said.

He settled into the passenger seat of my cargo van and we started down to the docks. I loved the city this time of day. The streets were quiet and dark, but it felt like the world was just on the brink of waking up. I got to see the sunrise every morning. The world is black and white in the dark, but as the sun rises it fills with color. That's a phenomenon I'd never get tired of.

"So where do you work," I asked, "that puts you out so late at night?"

"I'm a bartender, at the 31st Street Bar and Grill," he said, turning so I could see his shirt.

"Oh," I said. That didn't explain the expensive jeans. It also didn't explain why I could see the grey t-shirt that he had worn yesterday peeking out from under his work shirt. Didn't this man ever change clothes? It did explain why he would be awake at this hour, but it also presented a new puzzle. Yesterday he'd been awake at the same time, but not dressed in his work shirt and not reeking of beer like he was now. What a mystery.

"Oh?" he said. "That's the only response I get?" There was mischief in his voice.

"Yes, oh," I said, smiling in return. "Oh as in – Oh! You're a bartender for one of my competitors. You're probably tagging along to steal my trade secrets!"

He snorted. "I hardly think we pose much of a threat to you. From what I saw yesterday, your food blows ours out of the water."

"My food is pretty awesome," I teased.

"Well, now look who's all high and mighty." God he was beautiful when he smiled. "Of course it is true... You are amazing."

He meant my food. My food is amazing, not me. Time to change the subject.

"Have you ever been down to the docks for the morning catch?" I asked.

"Nope. First time for everything I guess," he replied.

"It's an experience."

"Really? How?"

"You'll see when we get there." I glanced over at him briefly before turning my eyes back to the road. "You asked me an awful lot of questions yesterday. Do I get to reciprocate today?"

"Nope," he said. "I haven't finished with you yet."

"I had a feeling you would say that."

We bantered back and forth like that, with me spilling my whole life out and him offering no information at all, until we arrived at the docks.

"This is our stop," I said, pulling the van into my usual spot. "Get ready for the adventure."

Fish Guts and Friendship

Jackson

"Alissa baby!" The man calling was not quite as big as Jason, but his arms were built the same way. He was tossing a watermelon from the truck behind him to one of his coworkers who was then stacking them in a display bin.

"Gary!" she replied. "How's my favorite produce man this morning?"

"I'm better now that you're here," Gary said. "Who's the eye candy?"

His eyes raked over me, but he showed no sign of jealousy or disappointment. I thought his relationship with Alissa was strictly business. I hoped she wasn't seeing anyone romantically, although now that I thought about it, I had never come right out and asked. That thought filled me with dread.

"This is Jackson," she said, snapping me out of my pondering. "Jackson, meet Gary. He's the man to see in fruits." She laughed, and her beauty suddenly stuck me. It was a grey and dreary morning, but looking at her smile made me feel like I was standing in the midday sun.

Gary gave me that overbearing big brother look. Apparently I was not the only one who felt protective of Alissa.

"Good morning," I said politely. He just kept tossing watermelons. No wonder his arms looked like steel cables. Forget the gym, I should get a job tossing melons.

"What's it gonna' be today, Alissa?" he asked.

She placed her order and Gary nodded at her. It was a big order, but he didn't write anything down. I wondered if he would get it right. She kept walking down the street, so I followed along. We repeated a very similar process with about four other vendors who were selling everything from produce to paper products. The last stop however was the biggest adventure of the morning. Alissa bought her fish literally right out of the ocean.

"Morning, Peter," she called to a tall lanky man who was dressed in filthy coveralls.

"Morning, Alissa. What's the special of the day gonna' be?"

"You tell me. Get anything good last night?" I got the impression that this conversation happened exactly this way every morning. I was so glad I'd come along. Watching her shop was like having a window into the first two hours of her day.

"Ayuh, I'd take the salmon today," he said, "although we did get some nice tilapia too."

He turned and whistled over his shoulder to another man who was standing about eight feet away pouring buckets of ice over huge tubs of fresh fish. The man nodded and then grabbed a massive fish from one of the tubs and tossed it to Peter. I'd never seen so much food thrown in my life. Amazingly, I hadn't seen one thing dropped all morning. Peter caught it, using a piece of newspaper like a catcher's mitt. He pulled the fish open so that Alissa could see the inside. It was a salmon, I knew, from the pink flesh. I had no idea that was what they looked like on the outside. That fish was huge! She ordered both, the salmon and the tilapia.

While they were packing up her order she walked over to the pier and looked out at the ocean. Her hair was taking on a reddish tint in the early morning light and framed against the water she was absolutely stunning.

"So what do you think?" she said to me.

"I think you're beautiful."

She rolled her eyes at me. "I meant about the market."

"Oh," I smiled. "It's pretty cool too."

Alissa

He is so beautiful and so infuriating. I wish I could figure him out.

We'd been walking around the market together all morning and his facial expressions had ranged from protective, to playful, to absolute awe, and even once, dare I hope, jealous.

It was clear that this was a new experience for him, but it looked like he was really enjoying it. I have to admit I was glad he'd come along. I wasn't above showing off in front of this man. I found myself hoping that I could somehow be worthy of him.

I had a hard time believing that he was really a bar tender. The beer smell, time of day, and t-shirt did seem to verify the information, but the way he carried himself, the words he chose, and his other clothes said otherwise. I was convinced that something wasn't right with what Jackson was telling me. Of course, he wasn't really telling me much of anything. Despite several attempts to pry for information, he always managed to turn the conversation back to me.

The more time I spent with him, the less I cared about the details. I just wanted to bask in his presence for a while - my own personal Bruce Wayne or Clark Kent. He could be a homeless bum for all I cared, and he'd still be perfect.

I stopped dead in my tracks.

Oh God. A homeless bum.

He had a bruise on his jaw, possibly indicating a fight.

"I'll take the tomatoes please," I said.

He was out in the open streets at odd times, in all kinds of weather, with no coat.

"And the asparagus."

He never changed clothes.

He ate ravenously.

"That should do it."

It was clear that he didn't or couldn't shave regularly.

He jumped at the chance to use my shower.

He didn't seem to have a car.

He said he was in transition.

It's not possible is it?

He couldn't possibly be homeless.

I watched him very closely as I made my way through my normal morning routine. Sometimes it can be hard to tell with homeless people. I had done some volunteering, cooking at a soup kitchen, and I knew that some of the men and women who came to eat there were dressed like any other person that you would see on the street. Some of them even had jobs, but the cost of living, addictions, or other circumstances made it impossible for them to find a stable home.

It was possible that he was living on the streets or in some kind of program, but I didn't think he'd been doing it very long, if at all. He had a grace about him that you didn't usually see in ordinary people and almost never in someone with that kind of life. This must be some transition for him if he was literally living on the streets.

My brain had gone on autopilot. I hoped that whatever I just ordered would make a good lunch special. I knew Peter would have said something if I'd asked for something too outlandish, but I couldn't for the life of me recall what I had asked for. I was absolutely stunned at my own revelation. It couldn't be true. Could it?

No. No way.

I was desperate for a change of subject. "So what do you think?" I asked.

"I think you're beautiful," he replied.

I rolled my eyes in an attempt to distract him from my blush. "I meant about the market."

"Oh," he said. "It's pretty cool too."

I sat down on one of the large rocks by the water and looked out at the fishing boats. Jackson sat down gently beside me.

"It seems like something has you distracted," he said.

"No," I said smiling. "I'm just trying to figure out who you are."

"What do you mean?" he asked.

"Well," I needed to choose my words carefully. "You're something of an enigma, Jackson. You carry yourself like royalty, but you work in a bar. You will give me no information about yourself. You show up at the oddest times and say the most perfect things. I just wish I could understand where you're coming from."

"Who do you think I am?" he asked with his signature smirk. God I loved that smile.

"You don't want to know," I said. "It sounds really ridiculous, even to me."

"No, tell me. I want to know what's going on in that pretty little head of yours."

"Well," I said, "I am torn between two theories. Either you're homeless, or your real name is Peter Parker and you've been bitten by a radioactive spider."

He looked at me wide-eyed for a minute, and my heart

stopped. Had I gone to far? Shit. I'd offended him. Then he burst out laughing, and I almost cried with relief. He wasn't angry. His laugh was so beautiful it made my chest ache.

"You think I'm a superhero?" he said, still laughing.

"Yes," I huffed indignantly, "I do. You're out in the middle of the night, you're wearing very expensive jeans which you seem to wear all the time like a hidden superhero costume, you inhaled my French toast like you hadn't eaten for a week, and your split lip makes me think one of the bad guys finally got a solid punch in when you weren't looking."

"You are entirely too observant, Miss Alissa," he said. "But, I'm not a superhero."

I noticed that he didn't deny being homeless. So maybe that really was the case. I wanted to ask him more about it, but the look in his eyes told me to not ask questions when I wasn't ready to hear the answers. I decided to let it go for now. When he was ready, he would tell me. I wasn't about to risk losing him over this. We would work through whatever it was in time.

"Come on. The orders should be ready by now." I walked back up the row of vendors in the direction of my van. They had already loaded most of the order and were just packing in the last couple of boxes. I turned over my shoulder to continue my conversation with Jackson and was startled to find that he was missing. I had been so lost in my own thoughts that I didn't notice when he'd wandered away. Where on earth did he go?

I squinted into the sunrise and looked down the row of produce-laden tables. He was walking up the street smiling. One hand was combing through his untamed hair, the other was holding a beautiful, red, gerbera daisy. We had passed the flower stand, but I hadn't even given it a second thought. Apparently Jackson had noticed.

"For you my dear," he said, holding the single stem out to me.

"You didn't have to do that," I said. I was moved. He'd remembered my favorite flower from yesterday's interrogation.

He just smiled at me and then looked to the van where the workers were shutting the back doors.

"Shall we?" he asked.

Too Much Information

Alissa

Jackson kept me sufficiently distracted on the drive back to my restaurant. I thought he was purposefully flirting as hard as he could to keep the discussion away from him. I wasn't sure what to make of it. Why would he feel the need to hide from me? Couldn't he tell that I would accept him, no matter what his circumstance? We all had ups and downs in our lives; I could deal with it if he was going through a rough time.

My eyes flitted to the daisy that I'd placed on the dashboard. So thoughtful. I wondered, though, what it had cost. It couldn't have been very much, but if he was really struggling to make ends meet, then every dollar was a big deal. I thought about whether there was some way I could repay him. Breakfast, I guess. He did like my French toast. That thought made me smile.

"So, you sticking around for breakfast?" I asked casually.

"You think I would miss out on a chance to eat your food again?" he joked in return.

We pulled into the alley behind my place. "Hey, look who

decided to show up today," I said.

Jackson looked out the window. "This is Matt?"

"Yep," I said. "Looks like you're off the hook today. My real employee is here, so you don't have to do his job."

I parked the van and we both got out. "Morning, Matt," I said.

Matt shot Jackson an unfriendly glare and then walked around to the back of the van. I asked Matt to bring everything in, and I pulled Jackson upstairs with me. Typically I would help, but I had a feeling that letting the two boys work together would be like asking them to get into a pissing match, and I wasn't in the mood to deal with it. I was really enjoying my morning with Jackson. I wasn't about let Matt ruin that for me. I paid him for his muscles, not his social skills.

"I'm just going to hop in the shower real quick," I said to Jackson. "You can watch TV or something for a minute okay?" I put the flower in a bud vase and set it on the kitchen table.

"Sure. I can amuse myself for a few minutes."

I walked quickly down the hall and pulled a towel out of the linen closet. I grabbed a change of clothes from the bedroom and started the water in the shower. I felt like my head was spinning. The last thing I wanted to do was embarrass Jackson, but I couldn't help him if he wouldn't open up to me.

I showered quickly and got dressed. I brushed out my hair and returned to the living room with it still partially damp.

"Do you like eggs?" I called. "I was thinking we could have… " I stopped short. My handsome, homeless superhero was fast asleep on my couch.

I stood still and watched him for a moment. He looked so peaceful, like a perfect statue, unmoving but still graceful. I had only been gone about twenty minutes. He must have been exhausted. I wondered where he was sleeping or if he slept at all. If he really did work in a bar, then it was possible he was up all night. Did he sleep during the day?

I had so many questions and so few answers. I checked the clock on the microwave. It was 7:30 already. I'd let him sleep until breakfast was ready, and then I would feed him and tell him he was welcome to nap in my apartment until he needed to leave. Would that be weird? Was that really what I wanted? I had no reason not to trust him, but if he actually was homeless, did I want him to get used to being able to sleep in my apartment? I liked him. I couldn't deny that, but I was hardly ready to let him move in.

I had never been so confused. There was no Emily Post etiquette for how to deal with your new homeless friend whom you weren't really sure was homeless and wanted to be more than a friend – maybe. What a mess.

Half way through cracking the eggs my phone rang. "Hi, Lexy," I said. "Sure, you can drop by. I wanted to see you anyway."

Jackson's messy brown hair peeked around the wall separating the living room and kitchen. I cut my best friend off. "I gotta go, Lexy. See you in a bit."

"Something smells wonderful," he said. "Sorry I dozed off on you – I haven't been to bed yet."

"It's no problem," I said. "If you wanted to take a nap here after breakfast, you're welcome to stay. I have to get to work, of course, but I'll be right downstairs if you need me."

"Oh, no thank you. I wouldn't want to intrude, and I have somewhere that I need to be around lunch time anyway. I'll sleep after that."

I released the breath that I had been holding.

"Okay," I said. I piled breakfast onto his plate and handed him a cup of coffee. I was relieved that we had mostly avoided that danger zone. It sounded like he had a plan for the day, so he must have somewhere to go. I hoped it was somewhere safe. I didn't want to see him get into any more fights.

Jackson

I woke up to the most wonderful smells of fresh coffee, eggs, bacon, and potatoes. Alissa was on the phone with someone. It sounded like she was expecting company from someone named Lexy. I shouldn't be intruding. She had a busy life, and I was showing up unexpectedly and making it more complicated. I would leave right after breakfast. I needed to go and see Jason anyway.

She served up a wonderful plate of food, but it was huge. I had eaten like a pig yesterday so she probably thought I could eat a dozen eggs by myself. I was now regretting that late-night burger because I knew that I wasn't going to be able to eat it all. I dug in anyway.

This girl was far too trusting. Did she really just offer to let me sleep in her apartment unattended? I was glad that she thought so highly of me, but we were seriously going to have to have a talk about stranger danger when we knew each other better. Why would she do that? She had made a comment earlier about my being homeless which I had hoped I'd diverted her from. She really was observant. She saw far too much. If she thought I was homeless, did she just pity me? Was she feeding me and offering me a place to sleep because she thought that I couldn't mange on my own?

That wouldn't do. I knew I'd been vague and unresponsive, but I hadn't expected her to think I was homeless. I didn't want to be her charity case. Of course, I didn't want to tell her how wealthy I was either. I just wanted her to get to know me without any kind of monetary assessment attached. Why was that so damn difficult?

"So, what are you making for lunch?" She gave me a blank stare instead of responding. "You bought all that salmon at the market. I was just wondering what the lunch special was," I clarified. I didn't want her to think that I expected her to feed me lunch, too. Could I possibly make this any worse?

"Oh," she said. "Salmon. Right. Um, salad maybe? I think

we'll do salmon salads?" It was as if she was asking me if that was an acceptable answer. I couldn't help but chuckle. I had no idea what was going on in her pretty little head. Couldn't she remember what she had purchased at the market?

"That sounds good." I finished my food. "Thank you so very much for breakfast, Alissa. I should really be on my way, but I enjoyed getting to spend the morning with you."

"Yeah," she said. "Me too." Her eyes showed a little disappointment when I said that I was leaving. I was delighted by it.

She walked me down to the door, and I pulled her into my arms to hug her good-bye. God, she felt so perfect like that, the gentle swell of her breasts against my chest, the wonderful smell of her hair as I pressed my lips to the top of her head. I wanted to hold her like that for forever, but Matt came around the corner at that moment, and I had to let her go.

"Thank you, again," I said as I let the door close behind me.

I passed a woman about Alissa's age with short blond hair as I was walking out of the alley. I wondered briefly if that was Lexy. I guessed I would be meeting her eventually, if she was a friend of Alissa's. I said "hello" on my way past, but didn't stop.

I had a lot to accomplish in the next few hours. I was going to find a cheap hotel to plant myself in for the day. I needed to rest and take a shower.

I checked my phone. There was a text message from Jason. He had his call with Nick scheduled for one o'clock today, and I needed to be ready to listen in. It was time to settle back into my corporate persona.

I replied to Jason letting him know that we would make the call from my hotel room, since I couldn't be seen in the office, and then I set off down the street.

Alissa

The backdoor swung open almost immediately after Jackson left, and for a moment I thought that he might have come back.

"Hey, Lexy," I said as my energetic best friend bounded through my backdoor. I was glad she dropped by. I really wanted to get her take on Jackson.

"What did he want?" she asked.

"What did who want?"

"Jackson Hayes. I just passed him in the alley. What did he want?"

"How do you know his name?" I was suddenly filled with dread. Lexy was practically psychic when it came to me, but she couldn't usually pluck people's names out of thin air. *I* didn't even know his last name.

"Everyone knows his name," she said. "He's the richest man in the city."

Revelations and Anger

Alissa

The world went fuzzy. The richest man in the city? She had to have the wrong man. That just couldn't be right.

"He's what?" I asked, backing into the counter and holding on for support.

"Geez, 'Lissa, do you live under a rock? He's the CEO of Hayes Industries. He's been on the cover of at least two business magazines, and there have been dozens of articles written about him. He apparently tries to keep a pretty low profile. His brother does most of the public stuff, but he's so easily recognizable with that wild dark hair and blue eyes combo. Really hot isn't he? How could you not know that?"

Lexy was never wrong about things like this. She paid very close attention to the who's who of the world. Her whole life involved keeping up with the fashion trends of the rich and famous. She wouldn't tell me this if she wasn't sure.

I stared at her, completely speechless.

Oh God. He must think I'm such an idiot.

"What did he want anyway?" Lexy continued. "Oh

my Gosh! Did he ask you to cater a party?! Can I do the decorating? You have to let me dress you. This is such a big deal. This could take your career to a whole new level!"

No. No. No. This can't be happening. Why wouldn't he say something? He probably thought I should know. What kind of a small business owner doesn't look at the cover of Business Week now and then?

Oh God. I was such a moron. I just told the wealthiest man in the city that I thought he was a homeless superhero. There is no greater mortification. Someone please shoot me now.

"Answer me Alissa! When is the party? How much time do I have?" She paused for a second and looked at me. "And why was he wearing that shirt? Was he trying to be incognito or something?"

I couldn't help it. I slid down the counter to the floor with my head in my hands. No. No. No. I knew he was too good to be true. I knew that no one as amazing as he was could ever be on my level. I made such an ass out of myself. Of course, he didn't want to sleep on my couch. He probably had a fifty thousand dollar sofa.

I thought I could impress him with a couple of pieces of French toast? I was so stupid.

"'Lissa?" Lexy was on the floor with me now, holding me as the tears came down my face. "Alissa, honey, what is it? What did he say to you? If he did something to make you sad, I'll kill him. I don't care who he is."

I couldn't respond. I couldn't even breathe.

At some point I noticed that my employees had arrived. They were standing awkwardly in my kitchen watching me sob all over Lexy. I couldn't bring myself to care. I just kept picturing that beautiful crooked grin and hearing his laugh in my head.

What was he doing with me? Did he just show up here two days in a row to humiliate me? Did he think it would be funny to go flirt with some stupid girl who can't even manage a crate of live crabs? Was he after my restaurant? I hadn't been open that long, but we'd gotten pretty good reviews. Maybe he wanted to buy me out. Why the hell would he tell me he was a bartender? The whole fucking thing made no sense.

Everything that I thought I knew about him, which admittedly wasn't much, was a lie. I had spent two fabulous mornings falling for a guy that I could never in a million years have. I hadn't known until this very moment how deeply I felt for him. You don't know what you have until it's gone, I guess. Not, that I ever really had him anyway. I could never have been worthy of him, and if I was honest with myself, I had always known that.

He said I was observant. He must have been cracking up inside on that one. Nothing was further from the truth. I was so clueless. I knew his jeans were expensive. I saw how he carried himself. Why couldn't I put two and two together?

I felt Lexy tugging me up to a standing position. I couldn't do it on my own, but she was pretty tough despite her size. She was giving directions to my employees. Part of my brain registered that Tyler was taking charge of the kitchen. Lunch would still be served on time.

Lexy dragged me upstairs to my apartment, trying to spare me any further embarrassment. I don't know why she even bothered. My mortification was already complete.

Jackson

I settled into the room and looked around. It was by far the ugliest hotel that I had ever set foot in. I had cheated and used my iPhone for a quick visit to Expedia. I rationalized it away, thinking that I could have done the same thing at the library; it just would have taken longer. The hotels were cheaper in the less desirable parts of town. I couldn't bring myself to stay at the hotels that rented by the hour, so I settled instead for a Days Inn that looked mostly respectable. The hotel cost $70 a night, and I had to pay an extra $10 to be able to check in at 10 am, instead of 3 pm. I thought it was worth it for the extra hours of sleep. I was working again tonight, so I thought it would be okay.

Between my late dinner, the hotel, the new subway pass, and the flower for Alissa, I had spent just over $100. I had $48 remaining in my wallet. I needed some clothes, a toothbrush, and a razor pretty badly, but I thought they could wait until after I got some sleep. I was exhausted.

I text messaged the hotel information to Jason, set the hotel alarm clock, and fell asleep on top of the blanket. When I woke, I was disoriented. It was 12:30. Jason would be here soon. I got up and went to use the hotel shower. The soap left my skin feeling dry and itchy, but I did feel cleaner. I didn't really want to put my dirty clothes back on, but for now I didn't see much of a choice. As soon as Jason left, I would go out for some supplies.

A knock came to my door a few minutes later. Jason came in carrying a takeout bag. I wasn't particularly hungry after the huge breakfast that Alissa had fed me, but it smelled good nonetheless. I insisted on paying Jason for my portion of the lunch, and then we settled in to make our phone call.

Jason called and after being put on a hold for a few minutes was finally transferred to Nicholas Carver. I kept quiet as Jason explained to Nick that he'd listened to the tapes and was very upset with me. I could hear the excitement in Nick's voice as he became more and more convinced that Jason and I were on the outs. Finally, Jason dropped the bomb.

"So the only thing I don't understand, Mr. Carver, is why you did not accept my brother's offer," Jason said. "He offered you more money, and any reasonable man would have accepted it."

There was a pause on the other end of the line. His answer would determine our next steps. I needed to know what he was after.

"I want to sell my company to Hayes Industries," he said. "Because I want a seat on your board, Mr. Hayes. I believe that you and I could take this business to a whole new level together if we were not limited by the restrictions posed by your bother. I think you'll find that the other members of your board agree as well. It is time for a new CEO."

Ah, so he was after my job. Well that made sense. If he managed to split Jason and me up with this ploy, then he could move right in during the disputes and take over a significant chunk of my business. That wasn't going to happen. I signaled for Jason to end the call, which he did diplomatically, without giving Nick any more information.

A comfortable silence filled the room after the line went dead. "I guess we know what he wants," said Jason. "I'm sorry I doubted you man. I had no idea he was that power hungry. What do we do now?"

"I guess we call a board meeting and cancel the negotiations. I don't want to have anything to do with him. Unfortunately, I don't think the rest of the board will feel the same way, which has me worried. I wonder what he meant when he said our board would agree with him. Do you think we have a rat inside the company?"

"I dunno man," Jason said. "I've always trusted the guys that we work with, but maybe it's time to buy some people out and move on. We can't let this kind of stuff happen. I'll call Ben today and see if he has any updates for us. What's your plan?"

"Well," I said, thinking it over in my mind, "I guess there is no major hurry. The board still thinks I am away in Hawaii, and we should probably keep it that way for now. Let's see what Ben turns up, and then we'll make a decision. If we bring this out in the open too early, I'm afraid we won't be able to sniff out the rats. There could be lasting implications from this that extend beyond the Carver deal."

Jason agreed with me, so we decided to wait until we had more information before proceeding. I needed to get some supplies, and I wanted to take another nap before my shift at the bar tonight, so I showed Jason out and agreed to meet with him again for lunch the next day.

I collapsed on the bed and let my mind run wild. Nick was trying to take over my business, and I couldn't even bring myself to care. My mind continued to turn back to only one thing: Alissa Allen. I couldn't wait to see her again. I felt so relaxed with her; it was like nothing else in the whole world mattered when she was around. I was beginning to worry though, about how she would react when she knew the truth of who I was. I wasn't going to be able to keep it from her too much longer. She had a right to know. If I wanted her to be in my life, then I needed to know that she could accept me, and that meant being honest about myself. I just hoped that she would understand. I never expected to feel this strongly for her. I never meant to deceive her either. I just wanted her to get to know me without all the hype. That was okay wasn't it? She was strong. She would understand. I would tell her tomorrow. I would go and buy a change of clothes, take a nap, work my shift at the bar, and then I would meet Alissa first thing in the morning and tell her everything.

God, please don't let her hate me for this.

Action and Reaction

Lexy

"Well, it's about time." Alissa finally accepted the warm washcloth in my hand and wiped her tear stained face.

She groaned.

"Are you going to explain to me what that massive over-reaction you just had was all about?" I asked.

"Over-reaction? You can't call it an over-reaction when you have no idea what's going on."

"Silly Alissa. Of course I can. Number one, I know you, and I know how you over-react. Remember that time in high school when you hid in the janitor's closet for two days because you thought Eric Lerner was going to ask you to that dance?"

She shot me a death glare, but she kept her mouth shut. She knew I was right.

"Number two, I spoke to you three days ago, and at that time Jackson Hayes was not in the picture, which means that you met him either today or yesterday. Nothing could have possibly happened in two days to merit that kind of reaction.

You're freaking out over nothing."

"I am not freaking out over nothing," she defended. "I am freaking out because I just discovered that everything I know to be true about that beautiful, funny, warm, thoughtful, homeless, superhero is a lie. I wanted it to be true, Lexy. I never wanted anything to be true so badly in my life."

I rolled my eyes; what a drama queen.

"Listen to me, Alissa. If I hadn't walked in here and told you who he was, you would be busy gushing over him right now. The only thing that has changed is that you know he has money. I know you well enough to know that the money doesn't matter to you, which means that it's fear that is driving this reaction. You're afraid that you won't be good enough for him, because you have always felt that way about yourself. So what if he's rich? Clearly you had a good thing going, and I'm not about to let you screw this up just because you've decided that he's out of your league. Now get your damn ass out of bed and explain to me how in the hell you met Jackson Hayes."

Alissa

God she's pushy. She's probably right though. I am being a bit on the over-dramatic side. I just… well, I don't even know. I had no idea that one person could have such a strong effect on me. What is wrong with me?

My head hurt from the crying, and I felt more tired than I should. I asked Lexy to get some coffee, and then I settled in to tell her the whole story. She remained pretty quiet through the whole thing, which surprised me, and then she studied me carefully for a few minutes after I finished.

"That has to be the most bizarre thing I've ever heard," she finally said. "Jackson Hayes in dirty clothes, smelling like a homeless shelter, and looking like he was in a fight. That makes no sense at all."

"I know, right?" I said. "He's a total fucking mystery. I was completely convinced that he was a homeless bum until you waltzed in here and told me that he was a billionaire."

"And he came back to go to the market with you today?" I nodded my head to show that she had it right.

"Well," she said thoughtfully, "there's only one logical explanation. When he met you, he was behaving like someone else – only God knows why - and he liked you more than he thought he would. He's afraid that he'll lose you if he tells you who he really is, so he's keeping up the pretense. He wants you to like him, and he's afraid that you'll reject him when you find out the truth."

I looked at her like she had grown a second head. "Lexy, that is the dumbest thing I've ever heard. First of all, why would he be pretending to be someone else? Secondly, he does not like me, he likes my French toast, and he probably feels sorry for me. And third, he can't possibly fear rejection. He could have any woman he wants."

"I'm telling you, Alissa," she said. "He would not have come back today if he wasn't interested in you. There are a lot of pieces to this story that don't make sense yet, but there's only one way to separate the truth from the lies. You have to make him be honest with you."

I stared at her dumbfounded. My head was spinning. Lexy thought he liked me, but what did she know? I couldn't just call him out on it.

"So here's the plan, Alissa. You're going to go downstairs and finish your lunch service. After that, you're going to let me dress you, and then you are going to march right over to Hayes Industries and demand to see him. If he can come to your business, you can go to his. You're going to walk right into his office and tell him to lay it all out on the table."

She was completely nuts. I couldn't do that. Could I?

I made my way back down to the kitchen with Lexy on my heels. The lunch prep was well underway thanks to Ty's leadership, and I was glad to see that someone had chosen a lunch special based on the available ingredients. I was still unsure of what I had purchased this morning.

Jackson had certainly done a good job of messing up my head. I couldn't devote any more time or energy to this. Lexy was right. I was going to have to face this straight on. As soon as lunch was finished, I was going to find the infuriating man and demand an explanation. I had let him into my life, and now he was going to let me into his. If he didn't want to see me again, then so be it.

I fell into my usual easy rhythm of cooking and directing. The mood was a little more subdued than was typical for my kitchen, but thankfully none of my employees felt the need to ask about my melt down this morning. The time passed quickly, and before I had a chance to blink, the lunch crowd was on the way out.

Lexy reappeared as I was making my way upstairs to change. She dressed me in a black pencil skirt, button down shirt, and a pair of three-inch heels. It was one of the nicest outfits that I owned. I didn't usually have a need for more formal clothes, but I was glad that she insisted on this. These clothes made me feel stronger and more mature. I might not be in his league, but I wasn't about to show up at his corporate office in my fish-gut shoes either.

I can do this. I can do this. I can do this. Fuck, I sound like the little engine that could.

As she was doing my hair, Lexy gave me directions. His office wasn't that far from here, but I didn't want to risk getting sweaty on the walk over. I would take a cab.

I took a deep breath and tipped the cabbie. I couldn't help but look up at the building as I stood on the sidewalk. The entire place screamed intimidation. The building was massive, and looking up at it made me feel about as big as an ant. So much for feeling powerful in this outfit.

I can do this. I can do this. I can do this.

My hands were shaking as I walked in the front doors. There was a receptionist at a huge wooden reception area. That seemed like an acceptable place to start.

"How can I help you?" she asked coolly.

"I'd like to see Mr. Hayes," I said.

"Which one?" Oh, right. Lexy said that his brother worked here, too. I wondered if it was a whole family affair.

"Jackson Hayes," I clarified. I was really hoping that it wasn't a family name. I had no idea if he was a junior or the seventeenth.

"He doesn't see anyone without an appointment," she said. "And, he's out of town until the end of the week."

"Out of town?" I asked rather abruptly. "Where did he go?"

She gave me a glare that stated it was none of my business. "He's been vacationing in Hawaii. If you'd care to leave a number, I'll see that his assistant receives it."

"He can't be in Hawaii," I said. "He was just here this morning."

"I'm sorry, Miss," she said, clearly dismissing me, "He's been out all week." She turned to the next person in line behind me and went on with her job.

Hawaii? What the hell? Apparently I wasn't the only one he was lying to.

"Miss?" A smooth deep voice rang out in my ear.

I jumped. Man, I was really on edge today.

"Yes?" I squeaked.

Before me was a man with military-short black hair. He was probably a few years older than me, but not much. He was dressed impeccably in a black suit. He was handsome, in a way, but his eyes had a wild look to them. I wouldn't want to meet him in a dark alley.

"I apologize for eavesdropping, but I thought I'd heard you say that you saw Jackson Hayes this morning."

He smiled at me, and I felt like Little Red Riding Hood.

All the better to eat you with, my dear.

"Um. I must have been mistaken," I said. "He's apparently in Hawaii."

"I don't think you were mistaken," he said, taking a step closer to me. "Where did you see him?" I stepped back. He was seriously invading my personal space.

"I'm sorry," I said. I didn't know who this man was, and I didn't know what his interest in Jackson was, but I wanted no part of this. "I'm afraid I need to be on my way."

I tried to brush past him, but he caught my upper arm and pulled me into his side. His breath was hot on my ear. "You will tell me where he is." His voice was cold, and his fingers were digging painfully into my arm.

"I don't know where he is," I stammered. "I'm here because I thought he'd be here. I swear I don't know anything. Let me go."

Apparently he believed me, because he was gone a moment later, and I was left with my heart beating wildly in the lobby of Hayes Industries. I practically ran down the front steps of the building and hailed a cab. This whole thing was getting crazier by the minute.

Jackson

When I brought my fresh clothes back to the hotel, I showered again. I was going to burn my jeans when this was all said and done. I had spent $42 on another t-shirt, socks, and boxers. I'd also bought a razor and another toothbrush. I hit up a second hand store for the cheapest pair of jeans I could find. They didn't fit the same way as my regular jeans, but I could survive for a day or two. *They were vintage right?* I couldn't quite convince myself of that.

I got in a couple more hours of sleep and let my mind roll back and forth between Nick and Alissa. At six o'clock a knock came on my door. I let Jason into my hotel room. He was followed by a huge man whom I could only assume was Ben.

"It's nice to see you again, Ben," I said. "Thanks for saving my ass the other day."

He smiled at me. "No problem, man. You were actually doing pretty well on your own."

We got down to business. Ben and Sean had been following Nick for more than thirty hours. They weren't familiar with all of the employees in our company, so they took pictures of every individual that Nick interacted with. They put the large stack of pictures on the bed, and Jason and I started to dig through them.

I stopped on a picture of Kayla. "Where was this taken?" I asked. Ben looked over the photo.

"That's his apartment. That woman went in about eleven last night and didn't leave until about six this morning."

"Kayla Craigan spent the night with Nick Carver?" I asked. Jason shrugged.

I went back to the pictures. From the look of things, Nick and Kayla were very familiar with each other. Ben had gotten pictures of them kissing several times, sharing cab rides, and eating together. When had this relationship developed? Was it before or after I asked Kayla to do the due diligence on his company? How long had she been lying to me?

"Jackson," Jason asked, getting my attention, "Do you know who this is?"

He was holding up a picture taken in the lobby of our corporate office. Nick had his hand on the arm of a woman with long brown hair. He appeared to be whispering in her ear.

Oh God. Alissa.

I couldn't breathe.

What was she doing there? Her facial expression in

the picture gave me no help. It was pretty much a blank expression.

Seeing Nick with his hands on her made my blood boil. Was he targeting her? How did he even know who she was? Oh, no, what if she was in on this? What if she was part of his plan to ruin me?

Jason was saying something, but it sounded muffled to me. I couldn't fully process it.

Why was she visiting my office? Was she looking for me? She was dressed like she belonged in a corporate office. Did she have a meeting with someone?

"Ben, what can you tell me about this interaction?" I asked. I was trying desperately to keep my voice under control. Judging by the look on Jason's face, I wasn't succeeding.

"Um," Ben said. He flipped through a book of notes. "She was talking to the receptionist, and then he walked up and said something to her. We weren't close enough to hear what he said, but the whole thing lasted less than thirty seconds, and then he took off. It's my opinion that she didn't know him. She looked uncomfortable with him."

I let out the breath I had been holding. She probably didn't know him. She wasn't involved in this. That meant that she was looking for me. Oh God, that meant that she knew who I was!

"When did this happen?" I asked.

"About four hours ago," Ben said.

"Who is she?" asked Jason.

"That's Alissa," I said. I felt so empty inside.

"Alissa? As in the most wonderful French toast in the world Alissa?"

"The very same. She knows who I am, Jason. What the hell am I going to do? She's going to think I lied to her. She's going to hate me."

Those We Ignore

Kayla

I sat at a filthy desk in Nick's warehouse trying to prepare the offshore accounts that we would need. As I waited for the page to load, I let my mind drift to the Hayes brothers. I had watched them last week in the boardroom as they argued in that playful way that they did. It was like they were in their own separate world when they got like that. Sometimes I wondered why they even had an executive board. It wasn't like they ever took our advice.

Jackson threw his head back and laughed. He really was a beautiful male specimen. He would have made a good United States President – tall, good head of hair, articulate. He was a beautiful creature. It was a shame that I had to deceive him.

I didn't want to do it, not really, but I'd been sitting in Jackson Hayes's shadow long enough. When I got the position on the board I thought I had made it big. I thought I would be part of the intimate group that knew what made him tick. I thought I would get to make important decisions, be a part of something larger than myself. You can imagine my shock when I found out that I was to be a glorified secretary.

"Get the due diligence for the Wesin deal, Kayla. Where's my report, Kayla? Are you sure these numbers are right, Kayla?"

I had a masters' in business management from a prestigious university. I was not a fucking administrative assistant. I hadn't worked this hard just to be ignored.

Nick was right. They didn't care about anyone but themselves. Hell, they didn't even notice anyone else.

I left that board meeting with a fresh stack of assignments that were just as demeaning as all the others. It didn't matter. The only thing that mattered now was Nick. He was going to screw the Hayes for more than one hundred million dollars, and then we would disappear.

It was about time.

Nick had grown on me slowly. I didn't really like him at first, truth be told. He had kind of a hard edge to him, but once you got past that, he was a great guy. He was ambitious, decisive, and attentive. He asked me out four times before I finally caved in and said "yes." That man didn't like to take no for an answer. I smiled at the thought. There was something to be said for persistence.

He was an incredible lover. He really cared about me. We would be happy together on some tropical beach with endless funds and no responsibility.

Granted, I had always wanted more out of life than to be paraded around in a bikini, but at least Nick would pay attention to me. He was going to marry me. We would have a beach wedding at sunset. It would be everything a girl could hope for.

Screw Jackson fucking Hayes and the horse he road in on. It was time that he learned some humility.

Confrontations and Conclusions

Jackson

Did you ever feel like you were on the brink of screwing up the best thing that ever happened to you? It was like Romeo and Juliet, one giant clusterfuck of miscommunication that was bound to end in tragedy. There was no way that I could make this right. There was nothing that I could say.

I was going to go over there, bare my soul to her, and then hope like hell that she would understand. I had planned to tell her anyway, not that she would believe that, but I really did want her to know. I just wished that I had been able to tell her on my own terms. Now she was bound to be upset and confused. How could I have messed this up so badly?

And Nick! What the hell had he said to her? If he did anything to upset her, I was going to kill him. Forget gathering more information, I would drag his ass in front of the board right now and flay him alive. Kayla, too, if it came to that.

Jason was driving me to her restaurant. It was almost seven. She was sure to be swamped with dinner customers. What terrible timing. I was supposed to be at the bar at eight, but I had no desire to be there. I needed to grow up and forget this whole ridiculous farce. I knew I couldn't play homeless forever, but I was terrified that I would lose Alissa if I gave it up. I couldn't let that happen. She was the first girl who ever meant anything to me. She hadn't even known my last name, but I felt like she knew me. I had to believe that she would understand, that she would accept me despite my deception. I wasn't giving up that easily.

Jason dropped me at the corner, and I jogged up the alley to the kitchen door. I knocked and an employee that I hadn't met answered the door.

"Would you please tell Alissa that Jackson is here to see her?" I asked.

He gave me an odd look and then closed the door and disappeared inside. I paced the alley nervously.

"How's Hawaii?" her sweet voice called. I looked up at her standing in the doorway. She was so beautiful it hurt just to look at her. She was still wearing the skirt that she had worn in the photo. I wondered why she hadn't changed. I had to physically restrain myself to keep from sweeping her into my arms and refusing to let go.

I couldn't read her expression. It was a mix of anger and fear and confusion all at the same time. I just wanted to make it better. I wanted to make her smile. "God, Alissa, I am so sorry. I was going to tell you who I was, I swear to you…"

She shook her head. "I can't have this discussion right now, Jackson," she said, cutting me off. "I have a restaurant full of customers, and I somehow managed to order the most bizarre combinations of foods at the market this morning, then one of my servers didn't show up, so we're kind of behind, and truthfully I just can't have a breakdown right now."

She took a deep breath for a moment, and I could see the tears in her eyes. "I am angry at you for deceiving me, and I am very confused right now, but I promised Lexy that I would hear you out. I will hear you out, but not right now. I can't do this after the day I've had."

She was going to give me a chance. She would listen to me. *Thank you, Lexy!* She was just asking for a little space. I needed to be reasonable about this.

"Of course, Alissa," I said. "You're being more than fair. Just tell me what time you would like for me to be here, and I'll be here. I promise, I'll explain everything."

"No," she said. "I'll come to you. The dinner crowd dies down around nine. I'll be ready around ten. Where will you be?"

I considered that for a minute. She might as well see the whole picture at this point. "I'll be at work," I said, "tending bar at the 31st Street Bar and Grill." Confusion flashed across her face. "Unless you want me to call in and say that I'm not coming?"

She sighed. "No. Don't leave the poor bar owner shorthanded. I know how it feels. I'll come up and have a drink when I'm done." She turned to go back inside. "You are one strange man, Jackson Hayes."

The door closed behind her, and I slumped against the brick wall. She said she was angry and confused. I could understand that. I was confused as well. At least she had given me the benefit of the doubt. She was willing to be rational about this. She wasn't throwing anything yet, and she was going to come to the bar later to be with me.

I walked out of the alley to the subway. I had a job to get to.

Alissa

Could this day get any stranger? Seriously? He really worked as a bartender? I guess he wasn't lying about everything then. I couldn't think about it or I would go nuts. I was going to stop making assumptions and wait until he had a chance to explain himself. For right now I needed to focus on filling the dinner orders.

I had to chuckle every time I looked down at the dinner specials. Jackson had me so damn distracted this morning that I'd purchased three kinds of lettuce, but no cucumbers, peppers, or really anything else appropriate for a salad. I bought a massive amount of tomatoes – hence the tomato soup and the sudden abundance of marinara sauce on everything. I had no idea what to do with the tilapia because I hadn't actually bought enough of it to serve it for a meal. It was a mess. I was never letting Jackson come on a shopping trip again. He was just too damn distracting.

The worst part was that I couldn't even mange to be angry. He swept into my life and turned everything upside-down in a matter of days, and all I wanted to do was finish the dinner service so that I could be with him. I was hopeless. I didn't care who he was, how much money he had, or why he was dressing like a hobo. I just wanted to be with him. The rest would sort itself out somehow.

Dinner dragged on even longer than usual, and it was already 9:30 when I marched my tired ass up the stairs. I took a shower and pulled my hair up. Forget the power clothes, I was going to be comfortable for this discussion. And I was damn well going to take advantage of the bar scene too; I needed a drink.

Lexy offered to go with me, but I couldn't deal with her right now. Truthfully, I didn't even want to talk. All I wanted to do was sit and drink and listen to what I was hoping was going to be a very logical explanation for why my whole life had changed over the course of two days.

I took a cab to the bar and tried to steel my nerves. What was the worst that could happen? We could decide that we couldn't get over this, and then we would never see each other again. I would go back to my normal pre-Jackson life. I didn't like that idea; in fact, thinking about it gave me an acute pain in my ribs, but that really was as bad as it could get. I would watch his career from afar, and he would forget about me.

A small part of me was hoping, though, that maybe he wasn't just slumming with me. Maybe he really had come back because he wanted to get to know me better. Maybe my breakfasts would be enough to keep him around for a while. I smiled at that. I wouldn't mind waking up with him at all.

I paced back in forth in front of the bar for a few minutes. It wasn't particularly crowded for a Friday night, which was good for conversation. It was now or never.

I walked into the bar and spotted him immediately. He was reaching up to put glasses away above the bar and his shirt rode up enough that I could just barely see a sliver of skin above his low rise jeans. Hipbones didn't come any sexier than that.

Focus, Alissa! You are not here to fantasize about his pelvic area.

I sat down at the end of the bar and waited for him to acknowledge me. It didn't take long. He was a pretty attentive bartender. He gave me the most beautiful smile when he recognized me. Relief crossed his face. Did he really think that I wouldn't come? I was later than I had said I would be, but I knew he would be here all night. I hadn't meant to worry him.

"What can I get for you, beautiful?" he said.

You. Just you.

"Um, what's your beer on tap?" I asked.

I settled on a lager and he went to the other side of the bar to get it. I really needed to focus. I was supposed to be hurt and angry, but I just wanted to watch him walk back and forth. He caught me checking out his ass, and I blushed all the way to my roots. Damn him!

He delivered my beer and gave refills to a group at the end of the bar. When everyone was situated he returned his attention to me. "Alissa," he started, "I can't tell you how sorry I am. I never meant for you to be involved in this complicated, confusing mess. It's a long story, but if you'll let me, I'd like to just start at the beginning and work my way through."

"I think that sounds like a great idea." I could tell that this wouldn't be easy for him, and I did my best to reassure him that I would hear the story the whole way through before passing any kind of judgment.

He started with how he'd tripped over the homeless man in the street that day. He described himself as pious and self-absorbed.

How could he have come so far in just four days?

I couldn't imagine him being so cold to anyone.

He told me about the bet with his brother, and I had to fight to contain my laughter. It really was ridiculous. Who made that kind of a bet? Jason sounded like a character.

He broke from the story to get me another beer and to check on his other patrons. When he came back, he told me about sleeping in the airport, looking for work, his struggle to get a social security card, and his first night in the shelter.

He really had gone through a lot in the first two days. I was a little surprised that he hadn't given up. He told me about the thief and the split lip. Finally, an explanation for the fight and the smelly clothes! He could have gotten hurt, though; he had really taken this bet to the extreme.

Then he told me how he felt the first time that he saw me. "My whole life," he stated, "people have judged me because of my family, my money, and what they think they know about me. For once, I just wanted to know that I could make it on my own. I wanted to know that people could accept me for who I was and not what I had. When you looked at me, I felt like you saw me, and not the man that everyone else sees."

I could feel the tears running down my cheeks.

I do see you, Jackson, and I want every part of you.

I tried not to interrupt. He needed to get this out, and I needed to hear it.

He told me about Jason and Ben.... and Nick. He also told me about the photo that he had of Nick and me, and I have to admit, I was a little freaked out by it. I was also relieved, in a way, that I hadn't really been alone. Nick Carver was seriously creepy.

He told it all the way through until the present moment and then left me to my thoughts while he cleaned up the bar area and poured a couple of shots for the group on the other side of the room. I was grateful for our current location. He had given me a ton of information to process, and I wasn't sure that I was ready to respond just yet. The bar was keeping him busy enough that we couldn't really get into a heated discussion. Lexy was right about me; I over-reacted to everything, but this was too important to me. I couldn't let a rash decision on my part screw this up.

I sat and drank until the bar was ready to close. Jackson and I had agreed to go have pizza when his shift was over and finish the discussion.

I'd gotten the time that I needed to process my thoughts, and I had a lot to say. I wanted to tell him that he was an idiot for endangering himself with a stupid bet. If he ever put himself in harm's way like that again, he was going to get more than a split lip from me.

I wanted him to know that I was proud of him for his accomplishments in his real life and in his life this week. I was sure that his brother was proud of him, too. It appeared as if he'd learned to see the world in a new way over the last few days. I didn't know him before this week, but the man that I knew was incredible.

I wanted to tell him that I didn't care if he was a billionaire or a bum. I wanted him either way. I wanted the man who sat barefoot in my kitchen with damp hair and a lopsided smile, humming around my French toast and asking me a ceaseless slew of questions. I wanted the man who stayed up all night working and then wanted to go to the market with me, just so we could spend a little more time together.

I watched him for another minute, but when they were ready to lock up, I decided to wait outside. The bar owner didn't seem too thrilled about having me there while Jackson finished his cleanup. He said that there was a park across the street, so I walked out into the cool night air, clearing my head.

I jumped when a strong hand, covered in a leather glove, smashed into my face, covering my mouth and nose, cutting off my scream.

He stood behind me, pulling me flush against his body and wrapping his other arm around my neck.

"I knew you'd lead me to him," he said, in my ear, just before my air supply cut off.

What's Most Important

Jackson

I felt drained. Physically and emotionally, this one was one of the most strenuous weeks of my life. Explaining my journey to Alissa had really brought it all home for me. In a few short days, I had gone from a corporate tycoon, to a homeless bum, to a regular guy working in a bar who was trying desperately to impress an amazing woman. It had been a lot to experience.

She had been incredibly quiet the whole night. No one could listen like Alissa, and it made me want to pour my heart and soul out to her. I was cleaning as fast as I could. I was excited to finally hear her thoughts on the whole thing. She hadn't walked out on me yet, and I took that to mean that she wasn't angry. She would probably tell me I was an idiot, but I could live with that. I would do it a thousand times over if it brought me to her door again.

I had it bad for this woman.

I had decided to let Buddy, the bar owner, know that I would not be continuing this job. All good things must come to an end. It really was pointless now that Alissa knew the truth, and I needed to return to my real life to deal with the Nick Carver situation.

Fucking Nick. I hadn't been sure how to explain that whole thing to Alissa. She knew pretty much nothing about my business, and I wasn't sure that I really wanted to go into detail, but she had already had one run in with him, and I wanted her to be wary. I didn't trust him or Kayla, and I wanted Alissa to know that. I didn't want her to be anywhere near them ever again.

I told Alissa about Ben and the pictures he had taken of her in the lobby of my building. I thought she might be upset that she had been followed, but she actually seemed to relax when she learned that she wasn't alone. That was good. Clearly Nick had put some fear into her. I thought that was probably healthy for the time being.

I also explained how Ben had gotten pictures of Kayla at Nick's apartment. I didn't want to frighten Alissa any more than necessary, but I knew that Nick could be ruthless, and I had worked with Kayla long enough to know that she could be incredibly aggressive as well. Now that I thought about it, they were a perfect match. I wondered how I had missed the connection. They had obviously been working together and planning this for a while. I was going to have to put an end to it very soon.

I put down the dirty dishrag and started to restock the beer fridge. It didn't matter right now. All that mattered was Alissa. I was going to buy her a pizza and listen intently to everything she wanted to say to me, and then I was going to throw her over my shoulder caveman style and drag her home to my penthouse apartment where I would spend the rest of the night worshiping her beautiful body and listening to her sweet voice crying out my name.

Well, maybe not. I was really trying hard to be a gentleman, but the more time I spent with this girl the more I wanted her. I hadn't had an appropriate moment to kiss her yet, but I had every intention of rectifying that oversight as soon as possible. She'd only been outside for five minutes, and I was already desperate to see her again.

When I was done with the beer, I called out to Buddy that I was leaving. He yelled back a "see you later," and I stepped out into the night. I crossed the street to the little park where I expected to find Alissa waiting for me, but the park was empty.

"Alissa?" I said into the night. There was no response. I scanned the street. Everything was still and quiet. "Alissa?" I called a little louder, trying not to let the panic creep into my voice. Where was she?

"Alissa is occupied at the moment." Nick stepped out from a clump of trees. Oh God. He had her in a headlock and she was clutching his arms, clearly unable to breath. Her feet kicked wildly, but she was unable to reach him. In his other hand was a sleek black pistol. The barrel of which was pressed to her lower back, right around the kidneys.

How could I let this happen?

"She's in good hands. You cooperate with me, and she'll be fine."

"I will not negotiate on this. Let her go, and then we'll talk."

I looked around. Where was Ben? Weren't those guys following him?

"I tried to work out a reasonable business deal with your brother, but it turns out that he's too loyal to you. So, I'll just have to make my bargain another way."

Alissa

Oh God. Don't pass out. Don't pass out.

A dark sedan pulled up to the curb and Nick dragged me towards it. A fierce looking brunet woman got out of the driver's seat and opened the back door so that Nick could force me inside.

"Get in the car, Jackson," Nick said before slamming the door. I made an attempt to escape out the other side of the car, but he never released his hold on me and my struggle only made my arm blossom with a fresh bolt of pain.

"It's nice to meet you, Alissa," the woman said, "the girl who finally got the great Jackson Hayes' attention. I've worked with him for more than five years, and the self-absorbed prick has never given me the time of day." There was jealousy and spite in her voice. "But I think he'll pay attention this time."

She worked with Jackson...

Kayla. This was Kayla.

Jackson got into the passenger seat while Nick continued to hold me at gun point.

"I know you're not stupid, Jackson," Nick said. "Which is how I know that you're going to behave yourself until we arrive at our destination. Take your cell phone out of your pocket and toss it back here."

Jackson did as he asked, and the phone fell to the floor in the backseat.

"Drive, Kayla."

The car pulled away from the curb. I tried to control my breathing. It was better now that I could breath, but Nick still had a very firm grip on me, and I wasn't about to risk getting shot.

A few minutes later, we arrived at a warehouse in the old industrial part of town. They hadn't bothered to blindfold us or try to disguise the location in anyway. A small part of me realized that we probably wouldn't be leaving here alive.

Nick pulled me out of the car, never taking the gun away from me, and Jackson followed us into the building like an obedient puppy.

A chair scraped across the floor. Nick sat down and then pulled me up onto his lap. The sudden movement was too much for my stomach on top of the fear. I turned my head to the side and vomited all over the bare cement floor.

"Well now," Nick laughed, "I can certainly see the attraction that Jackson has to you. That was very lady like."

He thought this was funny? This was like some kind of a sick game to him.

He pulled my hair back roughly with one hand and locked the other around my waist. I tried to struggle, but I could do nothing except lay limply against him. Kayla was now in my line of sight. She was sneering at me. I don't think she approved of my position on her boyfriend's lap.

Well, join the club. I don't like it much either.

"Now Alissa," he said "you're going to remain very still and do exactly as I tell you."

"Let her go, Nick."

"All in good time, Jackson," Nick said. "You need to make a few phone calls first. You're going to wire five hundred million dollars to the offshore accounts that you see listed there. Distribute the money evenly."

Kayla handed Jackson a white piece of paper from the industrial desk in the corner.

"You fucking bitch," he spat at her.

Nick dug the barrel of the gun into my throat, and I let out an involuntary squeak.

"I require your full attention, Jackson," Nick said calmly, as if he was really in the boardroom processing a negotiation instead of holding a gun to my head. "After you transfer the money, we will be borrowing your private jet. You will see us safely into the air. When I am sure that no one will be disrupting our flight, I will release Alissa back to you."

"Release her to me how?" Jackson asked.

I couldn't believe that they were even discussing it.

It won't come to that. You can't pay all that money for

me anyway.

I coughed. I felt light headed like I couldn't get enough air. None of this was making any sense.

I tried to stop when I saw the worry in Jackson's eyes, but I just couldn't control it. I was crying and gasping for breath. Nick pushed the gun up under my chin.

"Shut up," he hissed in my ear.

Oh God. This is what it feels like to die.

Everything after that happened in a blur. Jackson was running full speed towards me. I was falling. My head hit the concrete, and the lights went out.

The End of the Whole Mess

Jason

"Nick did what?" I said.

I got this crazy call from Ben telling me that Nick was holding Alissa and Jackson hostage. My head was still foggy with sleep, and Shelby was glaring at me for waking her.

I got out of bed and pulled on some clothes. "Yeah, I'll call the cops. Yeah, calm down. Where is he headed? Yeah, I have the address for his warehouse. I'll meet you there."

I hung up the phone. I was not looking forward to calling the cops. I had a feeling that this was about to get very complicated. I made the call anyway and explained the situation as best I could.

The cop on the phone suddenly got a lot more interested when I mentioned Alissa's name. He asked me repeatedly if I meant Alissa Allen, Mark Allen's daughter. I had no idea who her parents were, but I offered that she owned a restaurant, and apparently that was enough information. They were dispatching four officers immediately to the warehouse where we thought that Nick was headed.

I told Shel that I needed to take care of something with Jackson and headed out into the night. I took the Jeep. It was the most versatile vehicle that I had, and God only knew what I would be getting myself into tonight.

Part of me was really hoping that Ben was blowing this whole thing out of proportion. It was always possible, but my gut told me that this was serious. I had never seen him so worked up over anything. He usually showed very little emotion.

Apparently, Ben had been following Nick, as we'd asked him to, but when Nick parked himself on a bench across the street from the bar where Jackson had been working, Ben had taken the opportunity for a bathroom break. By the time that he had returned from the Wendy's up the street, Nick had grabbed Alissa and was training a gun on her.

Not seeing a good opportunity to intervene, he'd gotten in his car and was now following them through an industrial part of town. Nick had a warehouse in the area, which I assumed was their intended destination.

When I arrived, I spotted Ben's car up the street. I parked on the other side of the building and got out.

One of the warehouse side doors had been left open, and I could hear shouting inside. The police weren't here yet. I circled the outside of the building hoping to find another entrance. I didn't think bursting right into the middle of everything right now was wise. I slipped in through an open loading dock. The security in this place sucked.

I moved along in the dark trying not to trip over anything and alert them to my presence. Moving behind a stack of boxes, I could get a pretty good view of the situation.

Jackson was facing Nick who had his back to me and was sitting in a chair with someone draped across his lap - Alissa presumably. It looked like he had a gun in his hand, but I couldn't be sure. Kayla was standing between Jackson and Nick.

I nearly screamed when Ben laid his hand on my shoulder. I was very glad that I hadn't.

I was a good twenty steps from Nick's chair, but I was pretty quick for my size. I thought I could probably run full speed and tackle Nick before Kayla could alert him to my presence. It was a gamble though, especially for Alissa. I didn't want to hurt her in the process.

I heard sirens in the distance. It was now or never. Nick was about to be alerted to our presence either way, and I thought that it was safer to try to take him down now. Who knew what he would do when the cops came in with guns drawn?

I did my best to explain my plan to Ben with hand gestures, and he seemed to understand. He nodded that he was ready.

I took a step out from the boxes and sprinted to Nick. Kayla saw me about five steps in, but Ben was faster. He lunged at Kayla just as I was reaching Nick.

I went for the gun first, pulling it away from Nick. It clattered to the floor, but unfortunately, so did Alissa. Jackson was immediately on top of Nick, punching him repeatedly in the face. Alissa was crumpled up on the cement. She was bleeding pretty badly from her head.

"Jackson, get Alissa," I said.

He looked up at me with wild eyes, not really comprehending. When he looked at her bloody form, he let out a strangled cry and released Nick. He pulled Alissa into his arms and began desperately to try to wake her.

Kayla took off running, but I barely noticed.

Nick was still fighting, also trying to make a break for the door, but I caught him and pinned him to the floor. He was no match for my size.

It had all happened so quickly. I hadn't heard the cops arrive. They burst in and held everyone in place at gunpoint.

They called for an ambulance while Ben and I did most of the explaining. I was afraid that Jackson was in shock. He was rocking back and forth on the floor with Alissa in his arms. I had never seen Jackson cry like that. They were both completely covered in her blood.

A few minutes later, both Jackson and Alissa left in the ambulance. I stayed behind to help the police sort everything out.

It took us all a few minutes to realize that Kayla was no longer present. Ben had shoved her out of the way, so that we could get to Nick, but she had taken off running before the cops showed up. My attention had been focused on Nick. The police were mostly concerned with getting Alissa to a hospital. Somehow in the confusion, she had simply disappeared.

The police sent a car out after her, making the assumption that she couldn't have gone far. I was hopeful that she would turn up.

Alissa

Ouch. Somebody turn out the lights. I groaned. *My head is fucking killing me.*

"Alissa?" My angel's voice. *Jackson.*

His face came into view blocking the blinding fluorescents. His hair was a disaster. He had a bruised cheek, a cut above his eye that had recently gotten stitches, and a swollen lip. He never looked more perfect. He was okay. We were going to be fine.

"Alissa, can you hear me?" he said.

Yes, Jackson. I hear you.

My mouth was dry; I couldn't quite talk.

A doctor appeared. "Hello, Miss Allen," he said. "Can you tell me how you're feeling?"

He shined a pen light in my eyes, and I flinched away.

What's with the lights in this place?

I licked my lips. He turned sideways, and then held a cup of water up to my lips. Much better.

"Jackson," I breathed. He appeared at my other side and took my hand.

"I'm right here, baby," he said.

Baby. I like that. I tried to smile, but it hurt.

The doctor talked for a while. I had a concussion, and numerous bruises, and they had given me something for the pain that was making me feel a little loopy. That was okay. I would recover.

"Alissa!!!" I could hear him from the hallway. Oh no. Someone had called my dad. This wasn't exactly how I planned on having him meet Jackson. I tried to sit up.

"Stay still, Alissa," Jackson said. "We can move the bed if you want to sit up."

"Yes, please," I said. Jackson found the remote for the bed and lifted my head up so I could see. My dad barreled into the room in full uniform with his gun at his hip. Oh great.

"Alissa," he said, stopping at the foot of the bed. "Are you okay? What happened?"

Jackson cleared his throat to get his attention. "Chief Allen? I'm Jackson Hayes," he said extending his hand. My Dad didn't shake it. Not good. Jackson lowered his hand. He didn't seem to be offended.

"Sir, Alissa has been through a lot, and the doctor wants her to rest. I think it would be best if I told you what happened."

"It's okay, Jackson," I said quietly. "I'm fine. I just need a drink." Jackson brought me the water from the bedside table.

"You sure?" he asked me with concern in his eyes. "I think you should rest."

"I will in a minute," I said. I wanted my dad to like

Jackson; I wasn't about to let their first discussion be an argument over my safety.

I started by assuring my dad that I was okay. Then I worked backwards through the story explaining about Nick and Kayla. He already knew most of this. The police had called him en route to the scene. My dad was good friends with several members of the neighboring police force.

He told me that Nick was in custody. They were still looking for Kayla. Jackson stiffened beside me at the news. Apparently, he didn't know that Kayla had gotten away.

He wanted to know how I knew Jackson. I sighed. This was going to be interesting. I decided on the abbreviated version. I told him that I met Jackson at my restaurant. It wasn't a lie, but I felt guilty about it anyway. I didn't know what to do. Telling my dad that Jackson was my boyfriend would answer a lot of questions and make the whole thing a lot easier. The problem was, I didn't really know where I stood with Jackson. We hadn't quite gotten to that point in our discussion last night.

"I'm dating your daughter, sir," Jackson said, "or at least I would like to be." He smiled at me with a silent question in his eyes. I smiled back. Yes!!!

"Yeah, Dad," I confirmed. "Um, sorry I didn't mention it, but you know... it happened kinda' fast."

My dad looked Jackson over as if deciding how to pass judgment.

"He's right, honey. You should be resting." He came around the bed and kissed me on the forehead. "I'm going to go down to the station and help the guys with the investigation. I'm sure someone will be by later to get a full statement from the two of you. Do you need anything before I go?"

"I'm in good hands," I said looking at Jackson.

After my dad left, Jackson lowered my bed back down and pulled up a chair beside me. "I am so sorry, Alissa," he started. "I'll never forgive myself for putting you in danger."

"Shhhh," I said. "No, Jackson. This wasn't your fault, and I'll not listen to you apologize. Just rest with me." I tugged on his hand trying to move him closer while I made room for him beside me. He took the hint and climbed onto the bed next to me. He was on top of the blankets, but I could feel the heat from his body through the thin layers. He felt safe and wonderful. He put his arms around me and pressed his lips to my forehead.

"Sleep, Alissa," he said, and I did.

Building Trust

Jackson

I woke to the most wonderful feeling. Alissa's head was resting on my chest, and her hair surrounded me. She was so perfect. I could really get used to this. She was still sleeping peacefully, but a glance at the clock and the presence of a nurse told me that I needed to get up. I had a lot of things to take care of. I untangled myself slowly, trying to disturb Alissa as little as possible, and slipped out the door.

I called Jason first for an update. The press had gotten the police report, and he was scheduling a press conference for this afternoon to keep them at bay. I was not expected to be present. The plan was to sneak me home in the backseat of a nondescript car to avoid media attention.

I found her doctor and got an update on Alissa's status. If nothing changed, they planned to keep her until about two in the afternoon. The doctors said she would heal, but they didn't want her to be alone. It was not wise for someone with a recent concussion to go home to an empty house. I was certainly not complaining. I wanted to take her home with me anyway, but I had a feeling that she was going to fight me on this. I knew she had a business to run, and frankly, so did I. Jason could smooth things over to some degree, but if the media caught up with us, it would be a disaster. I didn't want to subject Alissa to that.

I made two other calls, one to my personal assistant, Angela, and one to my parents. I had some explaining to do.

Chief Allen returned just before noon. I left the room, making an excuse about wanting lunch. I thought he would appreciate some time alone with her, even if she was still sleeping. When I returned from my self-imposed coffee break they were talking.

"He hasn't left your side," he said. They were talking about me, and I realized that I was once again eavesdropping, but I was far too curious to care. "Are you sure that you know what you're getting into with this one?"

"He's great, Dad," Alissa said, "I mean, I haven't really known him very long, but he's been very good to me.

My heart sunk. It wasn't true. I had deceived her, practically stalked her, complicated her life, and inexcusably put her in danger. The truth was, I was very bad for her, and I hated that truth with all of my being. I wanted to be the man she deserved. I wanted to give her the every desire of her heart, but I didn't deserve her.

"He put you in danger, Alissa," Chief Allen said. He was absolutely right.

"No, Dad," she said sternly, "It's not his fault that Nick wanted his money. It's not a crime to be successful."

I couldn't listen to this. I cleared my throat and stepped into the room making my presence known. Her face lit up with a brilliant smile, and I knew in that moment that I wanted to spend the rest of my life making her smile like that.

"You're looking better," I said.

She ran a hand over her hair as if trying to smooth it. She blushed. I loved her blush, but I should have kept my damn mouth shut about her appearance. I hadn't meant to make her self-conscious.

"I spoke with your doctor a minute ago and he said that you could leave just as soon as he writes your prescription and gives you your discharge instructions." She looked relieved. "However," I continued, "you're not supposed to be alone for the next day or two."

Her dad was looking at me now. He knew something was up. He apparently had excellent intuition, which was a useful trait for a cop. I guess you didn't get to be police chief, even in a small town, without some skills.

"So," I kept speaking. I had a feeling this would be a tough sell, but it certainly wasn't the first time I'd made a sales pitch. "I was thinking that it would be best if you came home with me."

I looked at the chief. If I was going to get away with this I was going to have to appeal to his over-protective nature. "I have excellent security in my home, and until the police have Kayla safely behind bars, I would prefer not to take any chances. There is also the media to consider. I am afraid that this may have caused quite a stir, and I would hate for them to harass you while you are recuperating. I can provide you with privacy and security for a few days while the police do their jobs."

"No way," Mark interrupted, "you're coming home with me, Alissa." He put his hands on his hips, which incidentally brought his gun into view. I wasn't convinced that it was an unconscious gesture. He looked like a wild west gunslinger ready to defend his daughter's honor. I just wished the gesture wasn't directed at me. Truthfully, my feelings were probably identical to his – we both wanted the best for Alissa. I just had to prove to him that she was safe with me.

"Knock it off, you two," Alissa's gentle voice chimed in, interrupting our staring contest. "I'm not going home with either of you. I am going back to my home. I have a restaurant to run. It's probably in shambles, and I have a million other things to do. I will be fine."

Alissa

The nerve of these guys! Honestly, I was a grown woman, not a four year old. Did no one take my business into consideration? I knew that Tyler would do his best, but I hadn't left any money for him to do the shopping, and there wouldn't really be enough supplies to get through the whole day. My employees had probably just put a note on the door and closed up shop.

The idea of going home with Jackson was, of course, appealing, but not under these circumstances. I was not his ward to be guarded, and I was certainly not a charity case who couldn't manage her own life. He was not going to throw his high-priced security at me and sweep me away to some exclusive hideaway. I had a life to lead.

And my dad! One little trip to the hospital and he's ready to pull me out of my life and make me go back home. *I don't think so.* He was always a little on the over protective side, which never really bothered me before, but this was ridiculous. I was not afraid of Kayla. I just wanted to go home.

"Your business is not in shambles, Alissa," Jackson said, breaking me out of my internal rant.

"How would you know?" I said. Great, now he's going to tell me how to run my business. "I didn't leave any instructions. There is no food..."

"I hired a temporary manager for you. He can run things until you are ready to return to work."

My jaw fell open. "You did what?" I couldn't quite keep the anger out of my voice.

"I called my personal assistant, who contacted a chef that we use on occasion for formal affairs, and he agreed to manage your kitchen for a few days. They contacted Tyler, who I believe is your second in command, and he let them in to your business and got everything running. They will keep things going smoothly for a little while. You don't need to worry about your restaurant. I assure you this chef is quite good."

I was speechless. I didn't know whether to be extremely angry that he had made all of these decisions without consulting me or relieved that he'd just absolved every fear that I had about my business. "How are they paying for the food?" I asked. I already knew the answer, but I wanted to hear him admit it.

"I gave them a temporary credit card so everything will be recorded and accounted for. I will gladly pick up any expenses that they incur," Jackson replied. He looked at the floor. "I didn't mean to overstep my boundaries, Alissa. I'm sorry if you're upset. I just know how important your restaurant is to you, and I wanted to keep things going as normally as possible for you. It's my fault that you're in the hospital instead of working, and I don't want you to be stressed out over this."

My dad was staring at Jackson like he was from another planet. Apparently, neither one of us expected Jackson to be so proactive. Honestly, it was really thoughtful of him to go to all of the trouble. I just wasn't sure I could accept it. I was used to doing things on my own, and suddenly having help from a man with unlimited resources was a bit unsettling.

I opened and closed my mouth several times. I wasn't sure what to say.

"Alissa, please," Jackson continued, "don't be angry with me. I just want to keep you safe until this whole situation is resolved. Just stay with me for a day or two until we are sure that it's okay for you to be alone."

I sighed. He sounded so sincere that it was really hard to be angry with him.

Finally Mark chimed in, surprising me. "Alissa, I hate to admit it, but I think he's right. It seems like he's thought this through pretty well, and while I'd much rather have you home with me, if you won't leave the city, I'd feel better if you stayed with him for today. I'll have the local PD work with Jackson's security people to ensure your safety." He frowned at Jackson. "Actually, it's the least you can do for my daughter after getting her into this mess..."

"Dad!" I interrupted. I was stunned, to say the least. First he tells me that Jackson's right and then he starts verbally attacking him. This was making my head spin. I was still very tired, and I honestly didn't have the strength to try to fight.

"Okay," I said, "I'll go with Jackson, but I want to call to Tyler and make sure everything is okay. If your chef sucks and gives my restaurant a bad reputation, you're in trouble. And this is for today only. I am going back to work first thing tomorrow."

After a few more grumbling comments from my dad and a couple of outgoing text messages from Jackson, we had a plan. I would stay at Jackson's for the rest of the day and sleep over tonight. He would return me to my restaurant in time to do my shopping tomorrow morning. We were all hoping that they would catch Kayla between now and then, and Jason should have a good handle on the press by then as well.

The doctor released me. My dad and Jackson left the room so that I could get dressed. As I was pulling my shirt over my head it finally sunk in. I was going to spend the night in Jackson's apartment.

Home Sweet Home

Jackson

The whole way home I was nervous. I was so busy this morning making preparations that I hadn't really stopped to think about how she would feel seeing my home. Was she nervous? Was she going to take one look at my apartment and freak out? Why did I have to live so damn ostentatiously?

She started asking questions about my house on the way there and answering them became awkward. I figured I should be honest with her; she was going to see it for herself in a few minutes anyway.

"I own a building that used to be a hotel. We renovated it into apartments, and I live in the top two floors" I explained.

Her eyes went wide. "You have two whole floors of a hotel? And you live there all by yourself?"

Yeah, I know it's overkill and it's not half as comfortable as your cosy apartment. I'll move! Just don't judge me for this.

I didn't answer her. I just let the silence become more awkward. It got worse when she asked what kind of car I drove.

"I have a few cars. I'm actually a bit of a collector."

"Well that was cryptic," she replied.

It was clear that she was finally retaliating for all the questions that I had asked her the day that I met her. I deserved the inquisition, but I didn't like it.

What if she liked the bum and hated the billionaire?

I sighed. "My everyday car is an Audi S4."

"And your not everyday car?"

"I'll show you sometime."

How did you tell someone about your collection of sports cars without sounding like a self-absorbed rich prick?

We pulled up to my private level of the parking garage, and I helped her out of the mini-van that the hospital had provided for our getaway.

I looked down the line of cars. Why did I not realize how much material shit I had?

Could you make it seem more like you're throwing your money in her face? You are such a fucking show off.

I guess spending a couple of days as a homeless person will really make you look at things differently. What was I thinking when I bought all of these? I never even drove most of them.

She was going to hate it here.

"Oh, wow," she exclaimed, looking at the cars. "These are beautiful. Is one of these yours?"

One?

"Jackson?" she asked.

I didn't trust myself to speak. I felt like I was on trial. I considered lying, but I didn't think I could ever lie to this woman.

"Um. They're all mine, Alissa."

But, I'll sell them all if you don't like them!

Please like them. Please like me.

Alissa

I was trying desperately not to hyperventilate This was no big deal right? It was just an apartment.

Jackson's penthouse apartment, my brain reminded me.

Shut up.

He just feels guilty because he somehow thinks that it's his fault that Nick is a psychopath. He's just helping with the security for a couple of days. It's not like he's taking you back to his place after a date. There hasn't even been a date.

But he did tell your dad that he wanted to date you.

Yeah, but he was probably in shock - one too many hits from the crazy guy.

He held you while you slept.

But I practically forced him to, and *he was gone when I woke up.*

I looked around. I hadn't really been paying attention to where we were going. Jackson had this amazing ability to make me completely unaware of anything but him. The van pulled up next to the elevators and stopped. Jackson opened the door and put his hand under my arm to help me out.

"Oh, wow," There was a whole line of expensive sports cars on this level of the garage. "These are beautiful." Most of them were a shiny black or silver, but there were two reds, one yellow, and one blue. I was no expert, but I thought each one was unique. By the elevator were two more cars, a silver Audi, which I thought was probably Jackson's, and a black Mercedes.

"Is one of these yours?" I asked.

Jackson wouldn't look at me. What was up with him? He was usually so open and genuine with me. Did I do something to offend him?

"Jackson?" I asked willing him to look at me.

Finally he met my eyes. "Um. They're all mine, Alissa,"

he said quietly.

"Oh," I said stupidly, "of course."

Smooth Alissa. He told you he was a collector. It's no wonder that he's being uncommunicative. He finally realized how uncultured and beneath him you are. You don't belong in this world - his world. You never did.

"They're uh, nice…" I finished lamely.

Nice? Did I really just call his multi-million dollar sports car collection "nice?" You are such an idiot.

It was no wonder that he wouldn't tell me about his cars. Listing them alone would take an hour.

The elevator arrived. He slid a special key into the slot, which gave us access to the top two floors. The elevator stopped at the thirty-third floor for most people. Jackson had thirty-four and thirty-five.

He looked really tense. I had to stop this.

"Jackson, I'm sorry," I blurted out. "This was a bad idea. You clearly don't want me here, and I don't want to make you uncomfortable. Maybe you should just take me home. I'm sure that everything will be fine. I can have my dad get one of the guys on the force to stay with me for a little while if we need to…"

"You think I don't want you here?" he asked, finally looking at me. His eyes now looked panicked.

"Well, yeah, I mean… I know that I don't really belong in a place like this, and I am sure that you have a lot of work to do, and I don't want to intrude…"

He let out a nervous little laugh and then ran his hand through his already disheveled mess of hair. He was looking at me like he couldn't believe what I was saying.

He moved so fast; I never knew what hit me. One minute I was expecting him to stop the elevator and take me home, the next he had me pressed up against the wall, and his warm lips were pressing against mine. His hands tangled in my hair.

He was all I could feel. My whole body was alight with a consuming fire. He was all I could breathe, all I could taste. My everything.

He pulled away panting, his eyes still closed, and he rested his forehead against mine. "Alissa," he said, "please believe me when I tell you that I want you here."

The door opened behind Jackson. He still had his hands in my hair and his forehead pressed against mine. I could feel his hot breath against my lips. It took every ounce of my self-control to not tip my head up and recapture his lips, but I knew that we couldn't stand here in the elevator forever.

I had no idea what was going on, but as long as Jackson was saying that he wanted me, I wasn't going to argue.

"Um. Then are you going to show me in?" I asked sheepishly.

He backed away from me slowly, letting his fingertips brush against my chin. "I'm sorry, I'm behaving very rudely. I'm just a little nervous. Please come in."

I stepped out of the elevator into a foyer-like space. It had two plush leather chairs and a huge vase with a bunch of reeds in it. On the wall opposite the elevator was a door. It was only one door, but I was having a lady and the tiger moment. I had no idea what to expect on the other side. My head was still spinning from Jackson's kiss, and I felt completely off kilter.

Jackson punched a code into the keypad beside the door and then turned the knob.

"I would prefer that you not leave without an escort," he said, "but if you need to go in and out for some reason the code is 254772. I'll get you a key for the elevator. There is a pool and a gym downstairs on the second floor. The whole building is secure, so please make yourself at home."

He opened the door and motioned for me to follow him. It was every bit as beautiful as I expected it to be. Half of the top story had been removed so the dining room, living room, and library/music room had twenty-five-foot ceilings. He had a beautiful black three-quarter grand piano and shelf upon shelf of books. I could die happily in this room.

The huge glass windows looked out over the whole downtown area. I was willing to bet that this was considered one of the best views in the city. When Jackson stepped into my line of sight I was positive that I was correct.

"Um, please, help yourself to whatever you want," he said. His hands were in his hair again, and it reminded me of how it felt to have his hands on me. Just the thought made me flush with heat.

"The kitchen is this way," he said. I hobbled along after him. "I don't actually cook, and even if I did, I would be embarrassed by how badly it would pale in comparison to your food. So I think they stocked the fridge, but we can order in if you want something other than freezer pizza."

I smiled. "I happen to like freezer pizza." He smiled back at me, looking a little more comfortable.

The doorbell rang. "That'll be your clothes," he said. "Please excuse me."

My clothes? I heard Jackson open the door and greet someone. He came back in to the room with large grey suitcase in one hand.

"I hope you don't mind. I asked Lexy to pack a few things up for you. I thought you might like to have some of your own clothes for your stay. I would have just bought new, but I didn't know your sizes, and I wasn't sure what you would need or prefer…" He was rambling and it was adorable.

"Jackson?"

"Yes, Alissa?"

He looked like he was about to face a firing squad.

"Put the suitcase down."

He did as I asked. I leaned back against his kitchen counter.

"Come here." He took two steps closer to me. Close enough to reach.

I slipped my index fingers into the belt loops of his jeans and pulled him the rest of the way to me. I looked up into his beautiful blue eyes and then brushed my lips across his.

"Thank you," I said. I rested my head against his shoulder. His hands returned to my hair and he kissed the top of my head. "Thank you for thinking of everything, for taking care of my restaurant, for letting me stay here, for wanting to protect me, for getting my stuff."

"Shhh," he said, and then he was tilting my head with his hands, and his lips were on mine, and I could only be thankful for that. I opened my lips to him, and he gently explored my mouth with his tongue. He tasted like heaven, cool and sweet.

When he released me, I nearly groaned in disappointment.

Breathing Room

Alissa

"Let me show you to your room," Jackson said stepping back from me.

I followed him up the elegant open staircase. This place was incredible. The view of Jackson from the back as he ascended the stairs was nothing to scoff at either.

Damn it, Alissa. Get your head out of the gutter.

He led me past several doors and then entered a room at the end of the hall. He set the suitcase down on a small table in the large bedroom.

It was beautiful. The carpet was a neutral beige color, and the walls were a warm cream. The bed and the drapes were a study in blues. It was elegant, without being overstated. Abstract paintings hung on the walls, and I had a feeling that they were not replicas. I couldn't name the artist, but I would bet that any art student could.

"Is this okay?" he asked, taking in my reaction.

"It's perfect, Jackson. Who did your decorating?"

"What?" he teased. "You think I didn't do this myself?"

I laughed. "Did you?"

"No. My mom did. Interior design is her favorite hobby. She did most of the building. She's very talented."

A man who was proud of his mom, that was so sweet. "Yes, she is."

"Most of the rooms up here are just bedrooms, but my room is right across the hall, and at the top of the stairs where we came up, there is a study. You can use the computer in there if you want to. I keep all of my work stuff on my laptop or at the office, so there is nothing important or confidential on there. It's not used very much."

"That's very thoughtful of you. Thanks." Could this man be any more perfect?

"I'll just give you a few minutes to settle in if you want?" he said. "I was going to take a shower and then see about pulling dinner together. Do you need anything else?"

"No. Thank you, Jackson. Everything is perfect."

"You really like it?"

I laughed. "Of course I like it. This place is amazing." *Had he really thought that I wouldn't approve?*

"Good, make yourself at home. I mean that."

He left, and I dropped onto the bed with a heavy sigh. A shower sounded like a very good idea, but I wanted to see what Lexy had packed for me first.

A smile broke from my lips that I just couldn't contain. Fuck, he's reduced me to a silly, grinning little girl. I needed to focus. Honestly.

I unzipped the bag hoping that Lexy had made wise choices. I would need to call and thank her soon. I was glad that Jackson had spoken with her. She would be freaking out otherwise.

When I first looked in the suitcase, I thought that there had been a mistake. These were not my clothes. But, then I spotted my favorite blue long-sleeved shirt and realized what happened. Lexy bought me new clothes. That little brat!

I was afraid to look at what she had picked for me. Granted, everything she chose was always the height of fashion, but she was constantly trying to dress me in things that were girly and uncomfortable. Not to mention that she thought I should show a lot more skin than I usually did. She also spent too much money on me.

I sighed. Hopefully, she gave me my own underwear. She was always trying to get me to wear sexy underwear. I don't know why she bothered. No one ever saw them anyway.

No such luck. The whole side pocket of the suitcase was full of lacy, strappy, matching bras and underwear. God, she even packed me a practically see-through baby doll nightie. It was a pretty charcoal color, but I would be far too embarrassed to ever wear it, and I was sure that the occasion would never present itself anyway.

Well, a girl could dream.

I was still holding the nighty up when Jackson cleared his throat behind me.

"Oh Fuck," I blurted out. I dropped the lingerie and turned to see what he wanted. My face was burning. Why the hell didn't I shut the door?

He was laughing. That fucker was laughing at me.

"I'm sorry, Alissa," he said. "I just wanted to tell you that Lexy is coming over later. She was worried about you, and I asked her to join us for dinner."

"Good," I said. "I'm going to kill her."

Jackson

As I walked into my room, my phone rang in my pocket. "Hi, Lexy," I said. "Thanks again for getting Alissa's things for her."

"No problem. How is she feeling?"

"She's doing well I think. Would you like to come over and see for yourself? We're having dinner in about an hour."

We made arrangements for her to come, and then I called down to notify security to allow her through. I walked back across the hall to tell Alissa, and I stopped, stunned, in the doorway.

She was shifting through a pile of lacy underwear. I almost groaned aloud. My mind filled with images of her spread out on that bed in nothing but those thin scraps of cloth. When she lifted a sheer nightgown from the pile I was done for. Did she really sleep in that? What if she slept naked? I was so fucked.

I cleared my throat to alert her to my presence. I couldn't handle it if she inadvertently showed me any more of her lingerie collection.

"Oh Fuck!" She blushed redder than I'd ever seen anyone before. It was the most adorably sexy thing I'd ever seen. I laughed to cover my natural reaction, which was to growl at her like some kind of animal in heat.

"I'm sorry, Alissa," I said, trying desperately to control myself. "I just wanted to tell you that Lexy is coming over later. She was worried about you, and so I asked her to join us for dinner."

"Good," she said. "I'm going to kill her."

"Why?" I asked, focusing mostly on trying to breathe.

"These aren't my clothes," she said. "Lexy went and bought me a whole new wardrobe."

Ah, well that explained the embarrassment. Lexy had excellent taste as far as I could see. Bless that woman.

"I'll, um, just be in the shower, like I said before," I mumbled. There was no good way to end this awkward conversation. I practically ran from the room. Her ability to reduce me to a horny teenager astounded me.

I stripped off my clothes and stepped into the warm

shower. The hot water felt wonderful after the exhausting and complicated week. I allowed my mind to wander to thoughts of Alissa. She was incredible. Kissing her had been amazing. Her hair was so soft and so beautiful. And she smelled incredible.

There was no way I would make it through this night without absolutely attacking her. I lowered my hand to my cock, which was already erect and aching.

Fuck, she was beautiful. Her blush would kill me. I let my imagination fill with images of undressing her. I would kiss every beautiful inch of her as I worked. I wanted to put my hands all over her flushed body, explore every inch of her.

I stroked myself as the hot water cascaded down my back. I thought of her sweet lips and how her body responded to me as I kissed her. I rested my head against the cool shower wall and grunted my release.

I was going to be doing that three times a day if she continued to stay here.

I hurried through the rest of my shower.

Regardless of what Alissa had said about liking freezer pizza, I planned to make a better showing than that. I was going to order in from the best Italian place in town, and I wanted everything to be perfect.

I made my phone calls as I towel dried and got dressed. Alissa had seen me at some of my worst possible moments, now she was going to see me at my best.

She hadn't freaked out so far, even saying that she liked it here. Maybe this would be okay after all. I was going to impress these ladies if it was the last thing I ever did.

Lucky Elevator

Lexy

She had better not screw this up. I had packed for her everything that she would need. It seemed a bit excessive for one night, but I had a feeling that Jackson would find a way to make Alissa stay a few extra days. Call it a hunch.

Alissa had been asleep when I visited the hospital, so I wasn't sure that she even knew I had been there. I hadn't stayed long because I knew that my purpose was better served somewhere else – like the mall - but sitting in that room watching him watching her sleep had told me everything I needed to know. That boy was positively smitten, and I was going to do everything in my power to see that things stayed that way. Alissa had been alone for far too long, and Jackson was perfect for her. I had a sixth sense about these things, and I was never wrong. Those two were going to get a fairy tale ending.

I had offered to bring something tonight to Jackson's, but he had assured me that everything was taken care of. He seemed the type to be prepared, so I wasn't surprised.

I pulled my dress over my head. It was a little more formal than it needed to be, but I was hoping to make 'Lissa feel more comfortable. I hadn't actually packed her anything casual. She would have no choice but to look nice. I was not allowing her to run around Jackson's house in her holey sweats. I knew she would be mad, but truthfully, she should be thanking me. Everything in that suitcase would look fabulous on her. I couldn't have made it any easier.

I grabbed my new, and might I add adorable, bag and headed out to the car. This was going to be an awesome night.

I pulled out into the street just as the rain started. I knew that there was underground parking at Jackson's building, and I was instantly thankful. He was saving my hair. A sudden bolt of lightning flashed across the sky. It looked like this might be a pretty bad storm.

I arrived at Jackson's without incident and handed my ID to the security guard in the lobby. He gave me a key card for the elevator and told me to return it on my way out.

On the second floor, the elevator stopped and the hottest man that I have ever seen stepped in with me. *Wow. I hadn't seen that one coming.* He was sweaty, and there was a white towel thrown over his shoulder. I was guessing that the gym was on the second floor.

I wonder if I can get a membership or if it's for residents only.

His T-shirt was tight across his chest, displaying his well-defined pecs. He lifted his head to take a drink from his water bottle, and my eyes were instantly transfixed on the muscles in his neck while he swallowed, the way the sweat rolled over his collarbones, the hairs at the back of his head that were more curly when wet. God, he was handsome.

He finished off the rest of the water bottle in one long swig and crushed it in his right hand. He turned his head to look at the elevator buttons and caught me blatantly staring at him. *Oops.*

He looked a little surprised to see me standing there, but after a moment his face lit up with a brilliant smile that reached the whole way to his shining blue eyes.

After a surprisingly comfortable pause, he finally spoke. "I know I haven't seen you here before, because I would definitely remember you. Did you just move in?" As soon as the words left his mouth, he looked like he regretted them. Truth be told, it was a pretty bad pickup line, but he had spoken it so genuinely. I sympathized. I couldn't think of anything witty to say in his presence either. He was fucking adorable.

"I'm visiting a friend," I said, "but incidentally, I wouldn't forget you either."

He smiled again, and I had the urge to throw myself across the elevator at him.

"I'm David," he said, extending his hand.

"Lexy," I placed my hand in his. He lifted it to his lips and brushed a soft kiss across my knuckles.

"It's a pleasure to meet you, Lexy."

"You as well."

The elevator dinged, and the doors opened. I shook my head to clear it and looked at the row of buttons. We were on the thirty-fourth floor. Jackson's floor. We were so distracted that we had failed to push a button for David. He seemed to realize this a moment after I did.

"You're visiting Jackson?" he asked. His face fell considerably.

"Oh no!" I said quickly and a bit too loudly. "Well, I mean, yes and no." The elevator door tried to shut. I stuck my arm out quickly to keep it from closing. "I mean, I'm here to see 'Lissa, who is here to see Jackson."

"What?"

"Why don't we step out of the elevator?" I offered. I hoped that Jackson wouldn't mind us borrowing his foyer for a few minutes, but I couldn't have this conversation while trying to keep the elevator stationary.

We stepped out, and the doors closed behind us. "What I meant to say," I continued, "is that my best friend, Alissa, is visiting Jackson, and they very kindly asked me to come to dinner with them. So I'm here to see both of them really."

A door opened behind me. "Lexy? Who are you talking…" Jackson stuck his head out into the foyer. "Oh, hey, Dave."

I breathed a sigh of relief; at least they knew each other.

"Good to see you man," David said shaking Jackson's hand.

"Likewise," Jackson said.

"I missed you at the gym this past week. Where have you been?"

Jackson laughed. "You wouldn't believe me if I told you." He looked at me, confusion crossing his face. "How do you know Lexy?"

"Oh, we just met in the elevator," he offered rather sheepishly.

Jackson chuckled and then gave David a look that I didn't quite understand. "Well, I was just unpacking dinner and we have plenty. Why don't you join us?"

Oh God. He was inviting this glorious creature to eat with us. Squee!!!

"Oh," David started, "I, uh, really am not dressed for it. I mean I was just, you know…"

"You live two floors down," Jackson said, like it was the most obvious thing in the world. "Go change and then come back up." He took the elevator key from my hand and handed it to stunned looking David. "We'll see you in fifteen minutes."

With that Jackson pulled me through the door into his apartment, and my inner girl jumped for joy.

Jackson

Dishes. I know I have good dishes here somewhere.

I, of course, knew where the everyday stuff was, not that I even used those very often, but this was actually the first time that I could remember entertaining in my place. Was I really that anti-social? I would ponder that later. For now, I was on a mission to find the good china that my mother had hidden around here somewhere.

It actually was a shame that I didn't feed people here more often; I had a pretty good setup for it. My dining room table sat ten to twelve, so I ruled it out for tonight. Too big and too imposing. I usually ate at the island in the kitchen, which could seat four, but that was too informal.

My final option was a really beautiful smaller dining room set that my mother had restored herself. She had considered it a rescue project when she'd found it at an estate sale. It had been long neglected, but that was Mother's true gift. She could look at a piece of furniture or even a whole house and see the potential in it, no matter how bad the outward appearance. She was actually like that with people, too. She believed that enough love could restore anything or anyone. She was usually right.

The table and four chairs were in the back corner of my library, behind the piano, but I could pull it out into the middle of the room for tonight. It would be a perfect setting for the three of us.

I had just finished with the place settings when the elevator bell rang. Dinner was right on time. I had ordered a ton of food. It was way too much for three people, but I wanted to make sure that there was a variety to choose from. I had ordered several wines as well.

I led the caterer in and had him set everything in the kitchen. After he left, I set to work. I knew it wasn't going to be as good as Alissa's hospitality. Nothing could beat her French toast and cozy kitchen. But I wanted to show that I had put forth an effort. I wanted her to know how much I cared.

I uncorked a bottle of the red wine and let it breathe on the counter. I turned the oven on warm and slid the hot food into it. I put the salad plates in the refrigerator to chill. Was I forgetting anything?

A moment later the elevator rang again, and I heard voices in the annex. That's odd, Lexy hadn't mentioned a guest, although now that I think of it, it was rude to assume that she would not want to bring a date. Did Lexy have a steady boyfriend? I was missing so much information. Surely, she would have said something.

I opened the door and was very surprised to see David, fresh from the gym by look of it, talking to Lexy. How on earth did they know each other? I watched them interact for a few minutes and could see the obvious attraction that they had to one another. I knew Dave was single, and from Lexy's body language, I thought that she probably was too. It was unexpected, but they actually looked really great together. I didn't consider myself much of a matchmaker, but they had arrived on my doorstep already paired together, so I decided to run with it. I had too much food anyway, and this would hopefully make things more comfortable for Alissa as well.

I told Dave to go change and then pulled Lexy inside. I needed her help.

She looked around the apartment for a moment and then squealed and started clapping her hands excitedly. I wasn't quite sure what to do with that reaction, but she saved me by chattering on about how perfect everything was and how Alissa was going to love it. I was very glad that she approved. I was hoping that meant that Alissa would have a similar reaction.

Lexy helped me to set another place at the table for David, and she lit the candles while I finished getting the food ready to serve. From the sound of the water, I guessed that Alissa had been in the shower just before the food arrived. I expected her to come down any minute.

Dinner and a Storm

Alissa

I showered and tried not to get my bandages wet. The hot water felt exquisite after the traumatic experiences of the last two days.

Truthfully, I was a little disappointed when Jackson mentioned that Lexy was coming for dinner. The idea of cuddling on the couch and eating freezer pizza with Jackson had kind of appealed to me. I knew he was right though, Lexy would be worried until she got to see me in person. I guess I could share Jackson with her for a while. I was holding him to a one-on-one date soon though. I was really getting desperate to spend some time alone with him.

After Jackson had embarrassed the shit out of me, I had closed the door to finish going through the suitcase. I would never forgive Lexy for my choice of outfits for the night. I had finally settled on a knee-length cotton skirt and a simple white collared shirt. The neckline of the shirt showed way too much cleavage, and I would never be comfortable in a skirt, but it did look nice on me. As much as I hated it, Lexy did have good taste.

After what felt like an extremely exorbitant amount of time, I thought I looked presentable enough for dinner. I refused to put on shoes though. Those open steps were treacherous enough going up, I wasn't going to attempt coming down in heels. Lexy, of course, had not packed my Converse.

When I reached the bottom of the stairs, I heard voices. Lexy and Jackson. Sounded like they were waiting for me.

A bell rang. I had heard it several times while I was upstairs as well. I wondered what it was. Jackson answered my question in his next sentence.

"That will be David. Would you get the door for me please, Lexy?"

Lexy blushed. *Blushed. Lexy.* I was the one who blushed. I have never seen Lexy behave like that. And why was Jackson asking her to get his door? And who the hell is David? I swear, I take a shower for five minutes and I am totally lost.

Something smelled wonderful. Definitely not pizza.

"Jackson?" I questioned.

"I just wanted to make a good first impression," he replied. "How did I do?"

He had turned the lights down and lit the room with soft warm candlelight. The sky was growing dark outside the huge windows, and the city lights perfectly accented the feel in the room. The small table was set beautifully with elegant china. It wasn't overdone, but clean and stunning.

"It's perfect, Jackson," I whispered. I wanted to cry. He didn't need to go to so much effort. Didn't he know that I was already head over heels for him?

Lexy entered a moment later with a tall blond man behind her. Totally Lexy's type. Holy hell, was Jackson playing matchmaker? That didn't seem like him, but the man was dressed in khaki slacks and a blue button down shirt that looked fabulous on him. His hair was still wet. It was pretty clear that he had just showered and come up for dinner.

"Alissa," Jackson said, "I'd like for you to meet David, my neighbor."

"It's a pleasure to meet you, Alissa." David said shaking my hand. Lexy looked smug.

"You, too." I wanted to say something else, but I honestly couldn't come up with anything so I shut my mouth and focused on crossing the room to the table.

Jackson pulled out my chair. "Can I get you a glass of wine, Alissa?" he asked.

"Sure," I said smiling. "It smells like Italian, so red if you have it?"

"Of course. Lexy?"

"Red for me too, please," Lexy replied.

"I'll give you a hand," David said. The two men disappeared into the kitchen.

As soon as they were out of eyesight, I turned full force on Lexy. "What the hell?" I said quietly. "First, you pack me nothing but dress clothes, lingerie and high heels! And then you're all gaga over Jackson's neighbor. How do you even know him? And..."

"You look fabulous," she interrupted my rant. "And, you will look amazing in everything that I packed for you. Believe me. I know these things. You will be very glad that you have all of that stuff."

I tried to give her a disapproving look, but she held up one small manicured hand to stop me. "And I met Dave in the elevator on the way up here. Jackson was kind enough to invite him to join us for dinner."

I gaped at her like a fish out of water, but didn't have time to respond before Jackson and David returned carrying four glasses of wine and a breadbasket. Jackson set the wine down and returned to the kitchen, saying something about salad. Dave seated himself beside Lexy.

I sipped the wine. It was fabulous. I tried not to let myself wonder how much it had cost. "So Alissa," David said turning his attention to me, "how do you know Jackson?"

I took a deep breath. "Well," I said, "that's a very long story."

"But a very interesting one," Jackson said, returning to the table with chilled salad plates and a large bowl of a mixed greens salad. His smile was devastating. I was a bit surprised that I continued to remain conscious in his presence.

He sat down beside me and handed the salad across the table to Lexy to have her start. David was still waiting for an answer.

"Um, I own a restaurant," I volunteered, "and I was having a bit of trouble with some live crabs, and well Jackson kind of went superhero on me and saved my lunch special."

Dave quirked an eyebrow at me, and Jackson burst out laughing. After that, the conversation flowed freely. Jackson and I shared the telling of the whole story of the last week, pausing only to serve an incredible dinner, and as we finished I felt like a huge weight had been lifted from my shoulders. It was freeing to have it all out in the open. We had given them the short version, including the basic outline, but editing it to a manageable length.

"Well," said Lexy "that will be quite a story to tell the grandkids."

I shot her a dirty look. "Well what about you two?" I threw back at her. "That must have been some elevator ride."

David looked mortified, but Jackson was almost in tears he was laughing so hard. When he managed to get his laughter under control, he changed the subject by asking if we were ready for dessert. After the incredible amount I had eaten, I just wasn't sure it would fit. Jackson had gone all out ordering Lasagna, stuffed chicken breasts, wonderfully spiced green beans, salad, bread, and now dessert. Everything had been fabulous, and he had played the perfect host. Someone had taught him very well.

"I thought maybe we would move into the living room," Jackson said.

We all agreed, and I moved to the couch. Jackson brushed by me on his way back to the kitchen, and I didn't think that it was an accident. I hoped that he wanted to be as close to me as I wanted to be to him. The wine and good company had warmed me, and I felt elated.

Jackson brought coffee in an elegant French press and served it with the dessert, a rich chocolate mousse cake. What a way to get to a woman's heart. He settled beside me on the couch after a few minutes. Lexy and David were sitting no more than six inches apart on the loveseat across from us.

A brilliant streak of lightning flashed outside the picture window suddenly illuminating the city. It was followed moments later by a monstrous crash of thunder. I jumped, and Jackson slid his arm around my waist in a comforting gesture.

"David," I said, "what do you do for a living?"

David set his coffee aside. "I'm an investment consultant," he said. I gave him a look encouraging him to continue. "Essentially, I help wealthy people make wise strategic investments."

"That sounds fascinating, Dave," Lexy cooed. I wanted to hurl. Could she be any more obvious? Usually Lexy was on the standoffish side when it came to men. She was a big fan of playing hard to get. I had never seen this side of her, and it was kind of freaking me out.

"Who do you work with?" I asked.

"Well," David smiled, "Jackson for one. That's primarily how we know each other. I manage his personal portfolio. We became neighbors after we already knew each other. He told me about the remodeling project for this building, and I was very interested. I moved in shortly after."

"How did you get into that line of work?" Lexy asked.

David turned his whole body to answer her. Honestly, if those two leaned any more into each other they were going to smack noses.

"I am originally from Texas," he answered. "My family's had oil investments going back several generations. One of my uncles kind of took me under his wing as I was growing up and got me interested in stocks. It just seemed like the right fit for me in college, and then I took over most of the family interests and added a few additional clients along the way."

Our conversation was interrupted by the sound of rain falling in heavy sheets on the balcony.

"That's quite a storm," Jackson said. "Are you sure you want to drive home in this, Lexy? I would be happy to make up one of the guest rooms if you would prefer to stay the night."

Lexy looked from Jackson to David. She didn't speak for a moment, but I got the feeling that she was somehow communicating with David via ESP or something. Those two were really getting weird.

"No thank you, Jackson," Lexy said, not taking her eyes off of David. "I'll be fine for the night."

Wait. She didn't mean... she wasn't going to go home with him? She just met him. I mean Lexy had her fair share of one night stands in college. So did I, for that matter, but I thought she had outgrown that phase.

"Actually, I should probably get on my way," she continued. "I know Alissa needs to rest, and I have an early consultation tomorrow." I opened my mouth to protest and then thought better of it. Lexy was a grown woman. She could make her own decisions. I was going to hear about it in the morning though. If she didn't call me, I was going to break down her door.

"Thank you for all of your help, Lexy," I said instead.

"Of course, 'Lissa. Call me if you need anything. I'm glad you're feeling better."

"I'll walk you out," David said.

"It was nice to meet you, Dave."

"You as well, Alissa. Night, Jackson."

As Jackson showed them out, I made a halfhearted attempted at gathering up the dessert dishes and coffee cups. I didn't want Jackson to think that I was unwilling to help, but the good food and wine had made me sluggish. He returned a few minutes later.

"Just leave it," Jackson said. "I have a cleaning staff that comes in every day. They will take care of it tomorrow."

"Oh," I said dumbly. Of course, he has a cleaning crew. What doesn't he have?

"Are you ready for bed?" he asked. It wasn't really late. I knew that I needed to rest, but right now all I wanted to do was spend time with Jackson. It had been a lovely evening, and I wasn't quite ready to let it end.

"I was hoping for another cup of coffee," I said. "Would you like to watch the storm with me for a while?"

Jackson smiled and returned to the kitchen for the coffee. I made my way over to the wall of windows and looked out into the night. When Jackson came back, he moved the loveseat so that it was closer to the windows. He handed me my coffee and then turned out the remaining lights so that we could watch the lightning.

He sat down in the middle of the loveseat and then gently pulled me into his lap. I sighed contentedly and laid my head on his shoulder. My legs were draped over his, one arm was around my waist, the other resting on my knee. We sat like that quietly watching the storm and enjoying each other's presence.

I kept waiting for the night to get awkward, for me to realize how different Jackson and I were, but it never came. Truthfully, I felt at home here as much as I did in my own place. I put aside my feelings of inadequacy and decided that right now, for this one moment, I had a right to savor this night and this amazing man. I didn't understand it, but I was certainly enjoying it.

In the safety of his arms, I was content.

David

We made polite conversation through the evening, and with every passing minute I felt more and more attracted to the incredible creature that fate had placed in my elevator. Lexy. She was funny, genuine, interesting, sweet, smart, beautiful, energetic, and everything else I found desirable in a woman. I'd never met anyone like her.

I found myself moving closer and closer to her as the night wore on. It was like being distanced from her caused me physical pain. I knew that I should be nervous, as it was like a first date, but I wasn't. I was more comfortable with her than I had ever been with women that I'd known for years. I never wanted to leave her side.

The storm grew worse and worse outside, but I didn't even notice it. The whole world could fall apart for all I cared.

"That's quite a storm," Jackson said. "Are you sure you want to drive home in this, Lexy? I would be happy to make up one of the guest rooms if you would prefer to stay the night."

Wait, wait, wait. She couldn't stay here. She belonged with me.

Lexy looked at me, silently asking a question that she should never have to ask. Of course, she could stay with me. I never wanted to be without her. I smiled, trying to be reassuring without coming right out and saying it. I didn't want her friends to think she was slutty for going home with me. It just wasn't like that.

"No, thank you, Jackson," she said. "I'll be fine for the night. Actually, I should probably get on my way. I know 'Lissa needs to rest, and I have an early consultation tomorrow."

I offered to walk Lexy out, and said a polite goodnight to Alissa and Jackson. I had a feeling that I would be spending a lot more time with them in the near future. That was fine by me. They were wonderful people.

I took Lexy's hand in mine while we waited for the elevator.

"So.."

"So..." we both started at the same time.

"No, you go ahead," I said.

"I um.... I've really enjoyed your company tonight," she said.

The elevator arrived, and we stepped inside. I pushed the round 32 and then turned to face her. I cupped the side of her face in my hand and pressed my lips to hers gently.

"I'm not done with you yet, darlin'."

"I was hoping you weren't." She smiled up at me, and I was done for.

"I know it's fast, and please don't feel pressured, but I really would feel better if you didn't drive home in this rain. Stay with me."

She nodded, and my heart soared. How could one person make such a huge impact in only a couple of hours?

I showed her in, and she made herself at home on my couch. I got myself a beer, and she asked for water. I'd never seen someone so easy to talk to. I wanted to know everything about her. She chatted away in the most beautiful bubbly voice. I could listen to her for hours, and I did. We slowly slid closer and closer to each other as we talked until I finally had her where I wanted her, in my lap with my arms wrapped securely around her.

The talking naturally faded into kissing, and when I'd finally undressed her and joined her body with mine, I knew that this was it for me.

We never went to bed. We spent the whole night making love and cuddling on the couch, baring our souls to one another. I told her things that no other living soul knew about me, and I wasn't the least bit embarrassed. There was nothing that I could keep from her. My only fear was that this fog around us would break and she would suddenly realize that this whole night had been a crazy experience.

Nightmares and Break-ins

Jackson

Alissa was screaming.

My first thought was that Nick had somehow broken in, but I knew that was unlikely. I bolted from my bed and into the guestroom flipping light switches as I went. By the time I reached her she was curled into a ball and sobbing into a pillow.

"Alissa?" I questioned. "What's the matter, sweetheart?"

She turned her tear filled eyes to me, and I crossed the room to join her.

"It was awful," she sobbed. I was beginning to put two and two together as my sleep fogged brain cleared. She had a nightmare. Why hadn't I anticipated that? That was perfectly natural after such a traumatic event.

I lay down on the bed and pulled her into my arms. "Shhh," I soothed, "it was just a dream, baby. I'm here now."

She quieted as I rocked her gently. "Please don't leave," she begged. The desperation in her tone broke my heart.

"Of course not," I said. "Just let me turn out the lights. I'll be right back."

I walked back towards my bedroom to catch the light switches that I had hastily flipped on. I suddenly realized that I had been sleeping in only my boxers. Should I put clothes on before I went back to her? She had fallen asleep hours ago, in my arms as the storm died down. Acknowledging the fact that she needed to rest, I had carried her to bed, and then gone to sleep in my own room. She was still wearing the outfit that she wore to dinner. I hadn't wanted to put her in bed like that, but I wasn't comfortable changing her either.

I ran my hands through my hair. What a mess.

"Alissa?" I said, "would you like to change out of those clothes before you go back to bed?"

She considered the situation for a moment and then blushed furiously. "Um," she started, "do you think I could borrow a t-shirt to sleep in? See Lexy..."

I chuckled. We were back to that.

"Sure, why don't you just come to my room? I am sure we can figure something out."

She got out of bed and followed me. I pulled a t-shirt and pair of my boxers out of my dresser and took them to her. Her eyes were still red from the combination of sleep and tears, but she looked calmer. I closed the bathroom door so that she could change and then nervously paced my bedroom.

She looked adorable in my clothes. Her hair was wild from sleep, and I wanted to bury my nose in it. I pushed those thoughts aside and settled her into my bed. I turned out the light, and then crawled in behind her. I spooned up against her body and listened to her heartbeat as she fell back to sleep.

The phone woke me not three hours later, and I nearly threw it across the room. Alissa had shifted in the night and our limbs were tangled together in the most wonderful way. Her body was warm and soft. Her head rested on my bare chest, her hair fanned out around me. It was a perfect fit.

I checked the caller ID. Jason. This had better be

important. I tried to untangle myself without waking Alissa, but she opened her eyes beside me anyway.

"Jason," I growled into the phone. "I hope this is an emergency."

"I'm afraid it is," he said. "Someone broke into Alissa's place. Her restaurant has been vandalized."

"What?!" I shouted. "How did this happen?"

Alissa was now alert next to me and trying to listen to the conversation. I flipped it on to speaker phone.

"Apparently, someone came in through the front door. There was no sign of forced entry so the police think that they had a key. They walked right in, made a mess, and walked right back out."

"How bad is it Jason?" Alissa asked.

"Alissa!" Jason laughed. "You got to the phone awful quick. Is there something you two want to tell me?"

Alissa blushed.

"Shut up, Jason. How bad is the damage?" I demanded.

"You need to come down and see. It's pretty bad, but no one was hurt and I don't think there was anything irreplaceable that was damaged. Whoever it was didn't go upstairs, or couldn't get through the door to the apartment, so Alissa's stuff is safe, but the restaurant is trashed."

Alissa looked at me, her eyes full of tears. "We'll be down soon," I said, and then I closed the phone. I held Alissa to my chest for a moment, and then asked if she was ready to go. She pulled her hair into a messy ponytail and put on a pair of strappy sandals. She was still wearing my clothes, and I was enjoying seeing her in them far too much. Lexy really hadn't packed her anything appropriate for this, and we were going to her place anyway, so it didn't make much sense to change.

We took the elevator down to the garage. I had grabbed the keys for the Audi on the way out the door. I got Alissa settled in the passenger seat and then headed for her restaurant.

I could tell she was trying to be brave. So far, she had succeeded in holding back her tears, but her posture was stiff, and she was incredibly quiet. I needed her to know that I would fix this.

"Alissa," I said, after a few minutes of awkward silence. "I am so sorry. I know this has to be related to everything else that happened, and it's entirely my fault. I will pay to replace everything. We'll just buy all new tables and chairs and whatever else is ruined. I'll hire a company to come in and clean it up. We'll remodel the whole thing. I promise you, I will make this better."

After a minute she answered me and her tone was far more spiteful than I could have imaged.

"Is that what your parents did, Jackson?" she choked, half exasperation and half tears. "When you broke your toys they just bought you new ones and you thought it fixed everything? I've poured my whole fucking life into that restaurant. Lexy and I finished those tables by hand because they were cheaper unstained, and I couldn't afford them any other way. My father and his friends laid that hardwood floor one foot at a time. I picked each and every part of that place. My decisions, the sweat of my friends and family. Don't you fucking tell me that you can fix this with a blank check." She broke down into sobs, and it was all I could do to keep the car on the road.

She was right. I was an ass, a monumental ass. I bought and sold companies like she sold sandwiches. I didn't build my business with blood and sweat the way she did. I didn't understand at all. I couldn't replace the hours that she spent picking china patterns or painting the walls just the right color. I wasn't there when she opened the doors to her business. I didn't get to see how proud her father was that day. If I knew her at all, I would have known that I was sticking my foot in my mouth. I was making mistake after mistake despite the fact that I would do anything to make her happy.

"You're absolutely right, Alissa," I whispered. "I'm sorry that I keep screwing up. I can't make it better, but I will do anything you ask of me. I will be here for you whatever you need, and if you want me to get the hell out of your way, I will do that, too."

"I just want to get there," she mumbled. She looked exhausted.

I decided to keep my mouth shut for the rest of the day. This was her life, and I was still largely an outsider in it. I would wait until she needed me to do something. I would listen to her instead of jumping to conclusions.

We pulled onto her street, and I parked at the curb across from her building. There was yellow police tape across her door, and her father was standing out front. I took a deep breath.

Here we go.

I left her to her father. He was glaring at me. I was clearly making a wonderful impression on him.

At least she hadn't been in her apartment last night when they broken in.

I pinched the bridge of my nose with my fingers. This was going to be a very long day.

Phoenix from the Ashes

Alissa

My dad tried to stop me at the door, but even I could tell that it was a halfhearted attempt. He knew as well as I did that I was going to have to go in there eventually. I wanted to get it out of the way. Once I got past the initial shock, I would be able to focus on the next steps. I wanted to be on my way to a solution, and the first step to that was facing the damage.

I felt bad for snapping at Jackson. Honestly, I didn't mean it, but he had frustrated me with his quick dismissal of my concerns. Sometimes I just wanted someone to tell me that life sucks. I didn't want his money, and I didn't want him to feel guilty about all of this. I just wanted him to wallow in misery with me for a little while. Was that so hard?

I leaned back against the doorframe and surveyed the damage. Most of the walls were covered with red spray paint. It was clear that the goal was to paint as much of my restaurant as possible with profanities. Their vocabulary left something to be desired: cock-sucker, whore, and slut weren't very original.

They had overturned most of the tables and chairs and there was splintered wood all over the floor. A huge stack of plates was shattered in the middle of the mess which meant that they had been in the kitchen too. There were very few things that were untouched. I sighed and wiped the tears from my face with the back of my hand.

After a minute my father came to my side. He looked like he was having an internal debate on hugging me. We never really had a huggy-type of relationship. I stepped back, letting him off the hook.

"Do they know who did it?" I asked.

"No," he said. "Someone with a key, they think. Who had keys?"

I ran through the list in my head. "Um. Me, Tyler, Lexy, Matt. I don't know. I don't really think any of them would have done this."

"We should call them all anyway, see if anyone is missing a set of keys."

"Yeah, okay. I'll get their numbers."

I walked awkwardly through the destruction to the kitchen. Fortunately, they had kept most of the damage in the dining room. According to my dad a neighbor across the street had called the police when they heard the noise - probably the plates. It seemed like they only had time to smash one stack before the sirens had chased them off.

Truthfully, it could have been a lot worse. I could repaint the walls. I would need all new furniture - most of the tables and chairs were either broken or covered in paint - but that was really the worst of it. I could just order twenty-five new plates. I wouldn't need all new china, and they hadn't touched the glasses.

I pulled my employee records from the file that I kept in one of the kitchen drawers. I gave the appropriate numbers to my dad. He looked grateful that he had something productive to do.

I went back into the dining room and started picking up

the overturned chairs, collecting the ruined table clothes, and surveying the damage in more detail. After a few minutes I noticed Jackson following my example, his arms full of red stained cloth.

"Just make a pile for them here," I said, dropping my armful on the floor. We'll burn them when the police are done with the pictures of everything. Jackson nodded and added his to my pile.

"'Lissa?" My dad called from the doorway. "We might have a lead."

"Really?" I asked. I wondered if one of my employees knew something.

"Yeah. We called Tyler. He says he doesn't have his keys."

"Oh. Did he lose them?" I hoped not. That would mean that the damage could have been done by anyone.

"No. He says he lent them to Ryan."

Jackson dropped a chair behind me, and it clattered to the floor.

"Who's Ryan?" I asked.

My dad looked at Jackson. I looked at Jackson. Jackson looked like he was going to pass out.

After a minute he answered me quietly. "Ryan is the chef that I hired to help run your business until you were well enough to return. I am such an idiot. He would have known Kayla from some of our previous functions. I should have seen that. I didn't know that they were friends, but it makes sense for it to be related. I am so sorry. This is all my fault." He looked utterly defeated. "I just can't do anything right when it comes to you. I swear to you I'm just trying to help, and I just keep bringing more danger and destruction into your life. I never meant for any of this to happen. I should leave. I'll just go."

He looked over his shoulder at my dad. "Please, Mr.

Allen, if I can do anything to help the police, you have my number. I will do anything I can, please just ask. I can't tell you how sorry I am."

I sat down in one of my ruined chairs and laid my head against the table. "Stay, Jackson," I said.

"What?" he asked.

"I think he has the right idea, Alissa." my dad chimed in, "I can help you clean this up. We don't need him here."

"Dad," I said, "a little privacy please?" I didn't look up, but I heard his boots on the floor as he walked out.

"Jackson, come here."

He hesitated, but eventually crossed the room to me and pulled out the chair next to mine. He sat down beside me, and I lifted my head from the table.

"Jackson, I am going to say something to you, and I want you to not interrupt me okay?"

He nodded to show his consent.

"It is not your fault that you are successful. It is not your fault that people want to take advantage of your success." He looked like he wanted to interrupt, but I held up my hand to remind him that he just promised not to do that.

"You have been a victim of some terrible circumstances in the last few days, just like me. You are not at fault. I appreciate your trying to help with my business while I couldn't be here. It was very thoughtful of you to consider the things that are important to me. I appreciate your letting me stay with you. If not for you, I might have been here when they broke in, and I could have gotten hurt."

I reached out and pulled his hand into my lap, lacing my fingers with his. "Thank you for everything that you have done, Jackson. I am sorry that I snapped at you earlier. I hope you can understand the fear that I was feeling. I wasn't really angry with you, and I am not angry now. We don't even know what happened yet. The police will look into it, but it could be that Ryan had nothing to do with this. Either way, it doesn't matter. It's Kayla's fault or whoever made this mess, not yours. You have been nothing but kind to me, and I don't want you to leave. I need you to stay with me."

He looked at me with tears in his beautiful blue eyes. "I really don't deserve you, Alissa," he said.

"How about I get to be the judge of that?"

He gave me a weak smile. "What can I do to help?"

"Make a Home Depot run?" I asked. "I'll make you a list."

I got my grocery list paper from the kitchen and started making a plan. We would need new paint for the walls, a cleaner to get the paint off of the floor, probably new floor wax after that, lots of garbage bags, and a spare industrial broom would be good. It was a lot to think about. I settled on painting and cleaning first. I would think about the furniture later.

I was a little surprised that Jackson didn't argue with me when I told him that I was going to do the work myself. I was sure that he would have hired a team of professionals if I had left it up to him. Maybe my words in the car had affected him or maybe he was just tired of making mistakes. Either way, I was glad that we didn't have to argue over it. A little manual labor would feel good right about now.

The police finished processing the scene, and my dad convinced them to let me continue cleaning. I wanted to be back in business as soon as possible. Bad publicity like this could be really damaging for me. I wanted to be back up in two or three days if I could manage it.

I was pulling the police tape away from the door when Lexy showed up. She had an arm full of restaurant supply catalogs. She could be a pain in the ass, but I was so very lucky to have her.

Ten minutes later, Mr. Jennings, the owner of my insurance company arrived to appraise the damage. He made a slow circle around the place and then stopped to study the door. "Where did they break in?" he asked.

"The police think they had a key," I answered.

"Oh," he said. He finished his walk, and then sat down at the table beside me and filled out a form.

Jackson joined us a few minutes later carrying paint cans, rollers, brushes, and a whole pile of other supplies. My dad went out to help him bring it all in.

"Miss Allen?" Mr. Jennings said looking up from his form. "I regret to inform you that your damages will not be covered by your policy. Please sign here." He pushed the form to me.

"What?" I said, "I pay that policy every quarter right on time. I have insurance for this business. Why wouldn't it be covered?"

Jackson sat down beside me and looked at the form.

"There was no forced entry, Miss Allen. The policy only covers you in the event of vandalism to the outside of your business or for breaking and entering. We are not responsible if you do not lock your doors or use poor judgment with regards to keys."

"What?" I asked again. "How am I supposed to replace everything if it isn't covered?"

I was shocked. My insurance policy was not cheap; how could they do this? I didn't remember anything like that from when I had purchased it. I should be covered for this.

"That's not my concern, Miss Allen," he said, clearly dismissing me.

"May I?" Jackson asked, as he took the form from me. I nodded weakly.

Without that money, I couldn't replace the tables and chairs. Decent chairs ran about $250 each. I needed at least sixty of them. I didn't have $15,000. If I went to IKEA I could get some for less, but that would still cost about $3,500, and it would only be a temporary solution. Restaurant furniture had to be really sturdy to accommodate the volume and variety of customers.

I still needed tables and tablecloths. I wasn't going to be able to afford this. I was making money with my business, but I'd only been open a year. I had poured all of my savings into it just to open the first time. I didn't have any start-up capital this time.

Insurance was supposed to take care of stuff like this. I was covered for flood, fire, theft over $1,500, and vandalism. I knew I was.

"I didn't catch your name," Jackson said, looking up at the insurance man.

"Jay Jennings. Now if you would just allow Miss Allen to sign the form..."

"Nowhere in this document, Mr. Jennings, does it state that forced entry is required for an act of vandalism to be covered." The two men considered each other across the table.

"I'm sorry, who are you?" Mr. Jennings asked rudely.

"Alissa is my girlfriend," he answered. Girlfriend? I kind of liked the sound of that, and I couldn't keep the smile from crossing my face despite the awful mess I was in. "My name is Jackson Hayes."

Mr. Jennings paled and began sweating. "Mr. Hayes, I'm sorry I didn't recognize you."

Oh God. Here we go.

"Please answer the question, Mr. Jennings. Where does it state that forced entry is required?"

"I'm sure we can work something out. I mean, Miss Allen is correct. She does pay her bill right on time every quarter. We can surely make an exception this one time."

I had never seen a man sweat quite so badly.

Seriously? Jackson could do that with just his name? I

wondered if he was a customer at the same insurance company.

"I don't see the need for an exception. This policy states that these damages should be covered."

"Of course, Mr. Hayes. We'll have a check processed today."

Jackson looked at me and then looked back at Mr. Jennings. Jackson looked extremely pissed off. I didn't know what to do. I needed that insurance money, but I didn't want it to be because Jackson was involved. I just wanted what was rightfully mine according to my policy. I wasn't trying to commit fraud, but this is why I had insurance in the first place.

"Jackson, I just..."

"Were you just going to take advantage of her?" Jackson sneered. He was leaning over the table now.

"Of course not, Mr. Hayes."

"Then what exactly were you going to do? Why would you tell her that this wasn't covered when it clearly is."

"It was just a misunderstanding. I'm sure..."

Jackson turned back to me.

"How much money do you think you need? If you were to replace everything that was damaged, all the tables and chairs, new linens, new door locks, new curtains and blinds for the windows, and whatever else I might be missing? A realistic estimate please, not a conservative one."

I thought for a minute and scribbled a quick list using the prices in the catalog that Lexy and I had been studying. "Um, the tables and chairs are the worst of it," I said, "About $25,000, plus the other stuff. I would say it was $35,000 to $40,000 worth of damage, I guess."

"Alissa, I'm sorry," Jackson said. "I can't stand for this. I know I told you that I would let you manage your own stuff, and I swear to you, I am not trying to interfere, but this is just wrong. I can't allow him to take advantage of you like this."

"Mr. Hayes, I can assure you that we can resolve this, if the lady thinks that $35,000 is reasonable we will give her $40,000 just to be on the safe side. I'll even agree to freezing her rates for the next year so she won't see an increase..."

"Shut up," Jackson almost growled at him. "Is this how you treat all of your small business owners? I have half a mind to pull all of my policies with your company as it is. Don't make it worse."

The man shut up.

"Alissa, are you sure you won't let me help you? We could just forget this whole insurance mess. I'll give you the money and make them refund your insurance premiums for the last year. You can find a new company. You don't have to put up with this shit."

"I just want what is rightfully mine in my policy, Jackson," I said. "If it says that it should be covered, then I want them to pay me what they are supposed to pay me. I don't want your money, and I don't want theirs either if that's not what I'm covered for. I just want what they agreed to pay me when I bought the policy."

Jackson's forehead wrinkled in the most adorable way, and I fought off the desire to kiss it. "I want to see your appraisal guides," Jackson said to Mr. Jennings.

"Of course, sir, but they are at my office, I'll have to run and retrieve them."

"You came to do an assessment without any kind of documentation? What did you plan to do, just eyeball it, or were you really planning on screwing her out of everything before you even got here?"

"Mr. Hayes I can assure you..."

"Never mind. I trust Alissa's estimate over yours anyway. I should call my lawyer, but I know she wants this to be resolved quickly. According to her policy right here," he jabbed his finger at one of the papers, "you are to pay eighty-five percent of the total damages minus her $1,000 deductible, which you are going to waive just because you've pissed me off. We're working with a $45,000 figure, because I think she's underestimating, so that makes it $38,250. I'll expect a check for that amount within the next hour."

Mr. Jennings swallowed hard. "Of course, sir."

"Is that okay with you Alissa?" Jackson smiled at me.

"Yes," I said. "That's okay with me."

Work and Working, Fights and Fun

Jackson

True to his word, Mr. Jay Jennings returned not more than fifteen minutes later with a check for Alissa. I had been thoroughly annoyed with him when I saw that he meant to deny her the money that she was rightfully owed. I wasn't sure if he planned to take advantage of her because he thought she was not intelligent enough to know the difference, or because she was a young female, or just because he thought he'd get away with it, but I was not going to stand for that.

They say money talks, and in this case it was true. He obviously did not want to lose the large amounts that I paid him every year in insurance premiums. It was our standard practice to keep the successful businesses that we acquired running pretty much the way they were before we bought them, which meant that we kept the same insurance companies and policies, unless a need arose for a change. Several of the businesses that I owned used his insurance, but as they were adopted policies, I'd never met the CEO. What a scum bag. I was going to have to take a closer look at those papers when I went back to work.

I was pleasantly surprised when Alissa leaned over and kissed me as he walked out the door. "Thanks for defending me," she said. "You're like my own personal knight in shining armor."

I was beaming. I wasn't able to remove the smile from my face for the rest of the day. I had finally done something right, and even Chief Allen, who had overheard the second half of the conversation, seemed to be proud of me for defending his daughter. I hadn't seen his gun once since I got back from the hardware store.

Alissa had amazing friends. Lexy rushed off to buy new linens and drapes as soon as the check cleared. Tyler showed up an hour later with a truck that he had borrowed from his father so that we could haul the trash out.

When Lexy returned, she and Alissa picked new tables and chairs out of one of the catalogs and arranged to have them delivered. The one damper on the day came when they found out that she would have to pay nearly double to have the furniture rush delivered. She scheduled the regular delivery, which was a week, but she was clearly upset that they would not arrive sooner. I was on the lookout for ways to help, but I knew that Alissa would be mad if I paid for the rush shipping. I had to be a little more creative than that. So I called my assistant Angela and asked her to do some investigating for me. We owned several shipping companies and a lot of companies that shipped things all over the country on a daily basis. I was hoping I could somehow get Alissa's furniture to hitch a ride with a delivery that was coming here anyway.

Angela called me back an hour later and said that there was delivery made within ten miles of the furniture store today. The truck would be coming back empty tomorrow to pick up another delivery. Two more phone calls got me connected to the driver, who called me "a fool in love" but said he would be happy to help. He was right, I was a fool in love, and I was grateful for his help. One more phone call got the furniture packed up and ready to be loaded onto the new truck first thing in the morning. It only cost me a couple of minutes of my time, and Alissa would have her tables and chairs tomorrow.

I was going to surprise her with the news when the truck showed up tomorrow, but I was beginning to understand Alissa more and more. I didn't think she was too keen on surprises, so I decided to tell her now. I thanked Angela for all of her efforts and then walked back into the restaurant where they were diligently sweeping up shattered plates and broken furniture.

"Miss Alissa?" I called.

"Yeah?" she asked, brushing her hair out of her face as she looked up at me.

"I have some good news for you."

Her face fell for a moment, and she looked worried. I burst out laughing.

"I tell you I have good news, and you look like I kicked your puppy!"

"You didn't spend any money on me did you?" She visibly cringed.

"Didn't cost me a dime," I swore.

"Good, then what is it?"

"I found a spot for your furniture on a truck that was coming back empty." She looked confused, so I continued. "Your tables and chairs will be arriving tomorrow, free of charge. The truck had to make the trip anyway, and the driver agreed to go a little out of his way to get your restaurant back up."

I nearly fell on the floor when she launched herself at me. She embraced me in a warm hug saying, "Thank you, thank you, thank you," over and over again. I thought I'd died and gone to heaven. I held her for a minute, just breathing in her wonderful scent.

"Of course, I did promise the driver that you would send him on his way a few baked goods heavier," I teased.

"Free meals for all involved," Alissa said.

"Make mine French toast," I said softly, smiling into her hair. I'd give her a million years to let go.

We took a break for lunch around 12:30. Alissa made club sandwiches, and we heated potato soup from the restaurant the night before. We ate in her tiny living room upstairs.

"Mr. Allen?" I asked. "Have you heard any more from the police?"

He put down his sandwich and considered me for a moment. He could tell that I was trying to play nice, and I could tell that he was beginning to forgive me for our rocky start.

"They haven't been able to get a hold of Ryan, which is leading them to believe that he was involved. He hasn't returned to his apartment, but they don't think he's left the city. They are tracking his credit cards, and he's still using them around town. They have a notice out for his car as well. It's only a matter of time before someone spots him."

I nodded and went back to my soup. "And Jackson?" I looked up. "Call me Mark."

After lunch, I needed to go into the office. I hated to leave, but I did have a company to manage, and I could only put off real life for so long. I promised to return to help with the painting this evening. I ran home to shower and change. I packed a bag with clothes for painting so that I wouldn't have to go home before going back to Alissa's.

I felt high after such a great morning. I was upset that Alissa's restaurant had been trashed, of course, but it had opened a lot of doors for me. I felt like I was finally getting on the right track with her, and I was especially glad that her father was starting to not hate me.

I opted to drive the red Ferrari. I almost never took this car because it attracted too much unwanted attention, but today, I would deal with the stares and comments. I wanted the whole world to see how happy I was.

I said hello to Angela and retrieved my massive stack of

messages. I sat down with her and went over my schedule for the next week. She had done an excellent job of pushing back my meetings, but things were really starting to pile up. I was going to need to put in some extra hours.

After Nick's arrest, my team of lawyers had done some investigating into his business. My first task was to read over the report and determine if any further action needed to be taken. Turns out the company was pretty much bankrupt. Kayla had falsified the previous financial models to make it look like a successful company. We were terminating the agreement immediately. The company would probably close.

I now had an extra spot on my board to fill as well. Without Kayla, we would be short a buying adviser. I wasn't sure about Robert either. I hadn't really had time to consider that situation, but I was unsure if he had been involved with Kayla and Nick. I wasn't going to accuse an innocent man, but I couldn't very well allow him to stay in my company if he had been involved.

We had a long list of potential investors who would be glad to join our team. I would ask Angela to schedule some meetings for Jason and me in the next couple of weeks. I made phone calls for the rest of the afternoon and tried to get everything back on track. Before I knew it, it was after 7:00, and I was so far buried in my work that I didn't even hear Angela coming in to tell me she was leaving for the day.

Shit. I had told Alissa that I would be back in time to help paint. I threw my laptop back in my bag and left the massive pile of paperwork for tomorrow. Driving to her place felt surprisingly like driving home. I parked out front and walked through the door to warm sounds of laughter. I stood and watched as Alissa interacted with Lexy and her dad. They all had such an easy camaraderie with each other. I was insanely jealous of that.

Alissa looked up from where she was taping up the baseboard and smiled at me. "How was work?" she asked.

"It was good," I answered. "I'm just gonna' go change so I

can help okay?"

She pulled herself up from the floor awkwardly. "I'll run upstairs with you. I needed a clip for my hair anyway. It keeps falling in my eyes." Lexy gave her a funny look, and I wondered if I was missing some inside joke between them.

I followed her up and shut the apartment door behind me. Next thing I knew her soft lips were on mine, and her warm body was pressing me back against the door. I dropped my bag to the floor and circled my arms around her. After a moment, she pulled back and looked up at me with those beautiful brown eyes.

"Not that I'm complaining," I said, "but what was that for?"

"You look incredible in that suit, and I just couldn't help myself." She traced my jaw line with her tongue and then nipped gently at my pulse point. I groaned. Fuck she made me so hard.

"If you keep that up, we will never get your restaurant painted," I said breathlessly. Lord knows I didn't want her to stop, but her father was waiting for us downstairs, and we really did have a lot to do.

She brought her lips to mine again and then took a step back out of my arms. "Yeah, yeah, yeah," she said with a little pout. "Go change."

"Give me a rain check?" I asked, pulling her to me for one more kiss.

"Deal."

Alissa

Good God he was handsome. When I looked up and saw him in the doorway, I thought I might orgasm right there on the floor. We'd been in a hurry this morning, and he hadn't shaved. The five o'clock shadow gave him a rugged bad boy look, but the perfectly tailored black suit screamed of responsibility, and the combination of the two was going to kill me. He was positively lickable.

When he said that he wanted to change, my heart almost broke. Of course, he couldn't paint in those clothes, but I wasn't ready to let him take them off yet – well, unless I got to witness the removal. I made a stupid excuse to go upstairs, and Lexy knew it. *Busted.*

I couldn't take it any longer. I had to kiss him. He was like a drug - a very powerful and addicting drug. I was officially hooked.

When he asked me for a rain check I almost told him to forget the painting and take me now, but he was right. I would hold him to it though. Some day in the near future I was going to get that suit off of him piece by piece. He was too damn responsible for his own good.

An hour later we were all covered in paint. Jackson had started it by accidentally dripping paint into my hair from his position up on the ladder. I retaliated by running my brush all the way up his bare leg from his sock to his knee. He tried to chase me with more paint, but I, of course, tripped over my own two feet and fell into the paint tray, spraying Lexy and my dad with liberal amounts of Adobe Desert. It was an all out war after that. Thank God we had covered the whole floor with plastic.

We were all laughing hysterically and rolling around on the slick, paint-covered plastic when we heard a throat clear in the doorway. Lexy gasped, and I looked up. David was leaning against the doorframe shaking his head.

"You know?" he said. "Someone told me that you might need some help with the painting over here. I don't believe a word of it. You seem to be doing just fine on your own."

Lexy stood up and crossed the floor, miraculously avoiding falling down again. "David," she purred, "how sweet of you to join us."

David was enamored; he never even saw it coming. Lexy

threw her painted arms around him and knocked him into the wall, which was also covered in fresh paint. "Welcome to the club."

"Oh, you really shouldn't have done that," he teased.

I was really glad that Jackson had purchased way too much paint, because I think less than half of it wound up on the walls. In the end though, it turned out beautifully. We cleaned up the mess and hosed ourselves off in the alley. Tomorrow we would finish the floor, hang the curtains, and bring in the new tables and chairs. With any luck, I would re-open the day after that.

When they were dry and clean enough to go home, Lexy, David, and my dad all headed out for the night. The police were watching the building now, in rotating shifts, until Kayla was found. The locksmith had changed all of the locks, but we weren't taking any chances.

Jackson pulled me into his arms and kissed the top of my head. "Can I take you home now?" he asked.

"I am home," I said.

"I want to take you to my home." He lifted my chin and kissed me softly on the lips. "Please, Alissa? I don't want you to stay here until whoever did this has been caught." He smiled against my lips. "I also have a rain check to cash."

I was done for. How could I possibly resist this adorable, sweet man with paint still drying in his wild hair? I returned his kiss.

"Just let me get a few things from upstairs," I said with a smile.

Fast Cars and Slow Nights

Jackson

Alissa went upstairs to gather a few things to bring to my house, and I ran my fingers through my hair nervously. I suddenly had a whole flock of butterflies floating around in my stomach. We had technically spent the last two nights sleeping together, but this time when I asked her to spend the night it felt different, and we both knew it.

I didn't want to rush her, so I was trying to keep my expectations at bay, but I was so very ready for her. Rolling around in the paint with her had felt like one long session of foreplay after the searing kiss she had given me in her apartment, and my body was craving more of her attention. I remembered the look in her eyes as she had curled her fist around my tie and pulled me down to kiss her. My dick was stirring again, and I fought it down with my last once of will power.

She came down a few minutes later and declared herself ready to go. I helped her lock up and waved to the police officers as we crossed the street together. It was then that I remembered I had brought the Ferrari. Every fantasy that I had ever had involving Alissa and one of my cars flashed into my mind. So much for keeping my cock in check.

"Where's your..." Alissa started and then she stopped dead in her tracks and sized up my baby. "Yours?" she asked.

"Mine," I said. She didn't notice that my gaze was fixed on her and not the car.

A beautiful smile broke out on her face. "Wicked!"

I helped her into the car and reached across her lap to buckle her in, which we both knew she was fully capable of doing by herself. I allowed my fingers to rest just a little too long against her hip. God she looked hot in my car.

I jogged around to the driver's side before I could embarrass myself any further and slid in beside her. "Wanna see what she can do?" I asked.

"I'd love to see what you can do with her." I didn't miss the deliberate double-entendre in her words. I was never going to make it back to my place in one piece.

I started the car and focused on the purr of the engine. Hell yes! I loved fast cars.

"Hang on tight," I said, and we were off. I was torn between taking the scenic route so Alissa could see what my car could do and getting home as fast as humanly possible. My mind was made up when I felt Alissa gently rest her hand on my thigh. I would explode if I didn't get her back to my place immediately. The short trip felt like hours as her hand slowly slid higher up my leg, and my erection grew inconceivably harder. At the first red light, eight blocks from my house, I pulled her to me and kissed her hard. She whimpered into my mouth, and I failed to notice that the light had turned green. A car behind us honked, and Alissa blushed furiously. I felt like I was in high school again.

I pulled into the garage and parked the car in its usual spot. I opened Alissa's door and squatted down to her level. I couldn't keep myself from kissing her again, but the position was awkward, and I was too anxious to let it last long.

She looked nervous as we made our way over to the elevators. As the doors closed behind us she turned and gave me a small smile.

"I don't mean to make you feel unwanted," I teased, "But if I kiss you again, we won't make it out of this elevator."

Her warm laugh filled the small space, and she pulled her bottom lip between her teeth.

"Jackson, I, um... thank you again, for all of your help today."

"It was my pleasure," I gently stroked her cheek with the pad of my thumb. "I love spending time with you." I hoped that sounded sincere; I meant it with all of my heart.

She leaned into me and pressed her lips gently to mine. The elevator stopped a moment later, and I dragged her into my apartment.

Alissa

It felt incredible to be in his arms. He had the most graceful hands, and I was absolutely mesmerized as I watched them trail up my legs. My breath caught in my throat as he looked at me with lust-filled eyes.

He turned his body more fully to me and ran his fingertips up the length of my arm from my wrist to my shoulder. A trail of burning fire was left it its wake. He kissed me gently, and then pulled back just a hair and traced the outline of my lips with his tongue. Everything he did was too light, too gentle, and my body was screaming for more.

I leaned into him, trying to achieve further contact, but he moved away from me an inch at a time, baiting me into following his body, driving me mad with his resistance. He hummed softly as we kissed, exploring my body with his gentle hands, encouraging me to move with him.

It was like an exquisite torture, never enough. He lowered his mouth to my neck and sucked gently at the soft spot where my neck and shoulder met. I arched up into his touch, wanting more, begging him with my body.

"Fuck, Alissa," he sighed, "you are so beautiful."

In that moment, I believed him. I felt like the most beautiful woman in the world under his attentions.

Nothing felt better than this.

French Toast and Findings

Jackson

I woke up very early in the morning. The light was still grey out the window. I wasn't sure what had awakened me, but I knew what was keeping me awake now. Alissa had rolled over in her sleep and her legs were tangled with mine, her bare breasts pressed against my chest, her hair all over my pillow, surrounding me with her incredible scent. I was as hard as a fucking rock.

I couldn't help but touch her. I didn't want to disturb her peaceful sleep, but her body was warm and soft, and she called to me like a siren. I gently brushed the hair back from her face, touching the soft skin of her cheek. She was so beautiful. I pressed my lips to the top of her head and pulled her closer to me.

She stirred slightly. "Jackson," she mumbled, not waking. "Stay with me."

"Forever," I said softly into her hair.

Her sleeping body shifted and her smooth thigh came in contact with my aching cock. I suppressed a moan and tightened my hand around my pillow. She snuggled into my chest, and I stroked her back gently.

She was mumbling softly in her sleep, but I couldn't make out many of the words. I willed myself to go back to sleep. A few minutes later it became apparent that sleep would be impossible. She let out a sexy moan and rocked her hips against my leg.

"Tell me what you want, Alissa."

"I want you to love me," she said.

"I do," I whispered before claiming her again.

A while later, I collapsed in a heap on the bed next to her with a goofy grin on my face.

"Jackson?" she said, still out of breath.

"Yes, Alissa?"

"I'll make a deal with you."

"What's that?"

"If you wake me up like that every morning, I'll make you French toast every day."

I laughed and placed a kiss on her cute nose. "French toast sounds fantastic."

Alissa

What a way to wake up.

I regretted to admit that I needed to get out of bed and start the day. I really wanted to stay here and do that again... and again. I swung my legs out of Jackson's bed and hopped into the shower. I was going to use the guest room. If we showered together, I would never get him his promised French toast before he had to go to work.

We agreed that I would make breakfast at the restaurant, and then Jackson would go to the office. He was hoping to be done in time to help me move in the new tables, but I knew he had a ton of work to catch up on. I felt terrible for monopolizing all of his time. We dressed and headed out of Jackson's place.

"Which keys did you grab?" I asked while we waited for the elevator. I wondered if he had a car to go with every mood. It would be really helpful if I knew that he drove the corvette when angry or the Jag when nervous. Did he have an "I just got laid" car?

"Um, the Audi," he answered. "Did you want to take something else?"

"No," I said. "I was just wondering."

He considered me for a moment and then retraced his steps and picked up another set of keys. "You're right." He smiled at me. "We should take the Vanquish. I fucking love that car, and I never drive it."

"Jackson, I didn't mean for you to..."

"I want to, Alissa. I've learned a lot in the past two weeks, and my favorite lesson is that I took a lot of things for granted in my life. I am going to appreciate and enjoy the things that I have from now on and that means not letting those 460 horses sit idle."

I cocked an eyebrow at him. "Am I going to be able to get into this one?"

He snorted. "No, but I won't let you fall."

He helped me into the car as promised. "Thank you, Mr. Bond" I said as he shut the door, which then led to a discussion of how cool the 007 cars were, and how awesome the actors were, and what a womanizing asshole the character was. Those movies made my feminist-alter-ego cringe.

He hummed and moaned in appreciation of my cooking, which made me want to jump him again, but we both had other things to be doing today so I refrained. I kissed him good-bye a little while later and watched him cross the street to get into his sleek sports car. I wondered for the five millionth time what he was doing with me. He had it all: cars, money, class, looks, brains, and everything else you could want. It made no sense that he wanted to be with me, but still, I would not look a gift horse in the mouth. I would enjoy it for as long as he would have me.

I cleaned up the breakfast dishes and spent a little time doing laundry and other everyday tasks that I hadn't had much time for lately. I knew things would only get busier when I reopened the restaurant.

The new paint was dry in the dining room so I removed the painter's tape and cleared away the plastic. One more good cleaning of the floor and we would be ready to move the new furniture in. I was still heartbroken over the vandalism, but I had to admit that the new look was going to be incredible. I was excited to reopen and see what the public thought.

Around 11:00 my phone rang, and I hobbled across the wet floor to get it.

"Dad?" I asked.

"Alissa," he said, "I have news. The local PD picked up Ryan this morning. He confessed to vandalizing your restaurant. He was connected with Kayla."

"Did they get her, too?"

"No, she wasn't with him. They are still looking for her. She was supposedly involved in the vandalism as well."

"Okay. Do the police need me to do anything?"

"No, just stay put, I'll be in touch when I have more information."

"Okay, thanks Dad."

"Sure Sweetie. What time is the truck coming? I'll help unload."

"They said around 2:00. I'll see you then?"

"Yeah. Bye, Alissa."

"Bye, Dad."

That was a typical phone conversation with my dad, straight to the point. I let out a deep breath. I couldn't wait until this whole thing was resolved. I just wanted to go back to normal. Well, normal plus Jackson. I would take on a million Kaylas if I got to keep him, but it was still stressful not knowing if my restaurant was really safe. Even if they caught her, we would be battling all of this out in court for a while, too. Just the thought of it was exhausting.

I returned to scrubbing the floor. The paint was almost all gone; just a faint hint of their sloppy scrawl was left. No one would ever know the difference.

I heard the backdoor squeak open.

"I'm in here, Tyler," I called.

I froze. It sounded like high heels clicking across the floor.

"Do I look like Tyler to you?"

Surprise After Surprise

Alissa

I swung around, trying not to slip on the wet floor.

"Fuck! Lexy! You scared the shit out of me."

"Geez, chill out. You knew I was coming over to help you hang the new curtains."

I took a couple of deep breaths. "Of course, Lex, I'm sorry. I just got off the phone with my dad, and I was thinking about Kayla, and I thought you were her. Paranoid moment." I breathed a sigh of relief.

"What's the latest news?"

I filled her in about Ryan's arrest while we finished the floor. All that was left were curtains and furniture. I was stoked.

As expected, Tyler showed up a little while later and helped to reach some of the tall things that Lexy and I couldn't get. I wasn't dumb enough to try to get on a ladder with my clumsy feet.

Tyler and I made lunch together while Lexy finished up in

the dining room, and it felt awesome to get back into a cooking rhythm with him. So much had happened in the last week, and I really needed this feeling of normalcy.

Lexy filled me in on all the David gossip. It sounded like the two of them were really hitting it off. They had been seeing a lot of each other. Lexy got this dreamy look on her face when she talked about him, and I recognized the emotion immediately. I recognized it, because I saw it on my own face every time I looked in the mirror. She was a woman in love.

As I listened to Lexy prattle on about him, I realized that I hadn't ever told Jackson how I felt. We'd had a lot of deep conversations – like the night in the bar, when he told me about the homeless week and all the things he'd learned, or the night of the storm when he held me and we discussed art, philosophy, and life in general, but we hadn't talked very much about us. I was content to just take things one day at a time, but I wanted Jackson to know how strong my feelings were. I hadn't taken the time to admit it to myself, but I was in love with him. I was hopelessly head over heels, and I loved every minute of it.

I couldn't keep the goofy smile from spreading across my face. I really needed to get some more alone time with that boy... man... my thoughts wandered back to last night... and this morning... definitely all man.

"I'm sorry, Lexy, what did you say?"

She just laughed at me, and then asked me to hand her a different screwdriver. She couldn't make fun of me because she was just as over the moon as I was.

My dad showed up around 2:00, and Jackson showed up at 2:30. The truck was late. At 3:00, Jackson suggested that we try to get the truck driver on the phone. There was no answer on his cell. At 3:30 the truck finally pulled up into the alley. We all went out into the side alley to greet the driver and help bring in the furniture. What met us, however, was not the truck driver we had expected.

Her eyes were bloodshot like she hadn't had a good night's

sleep in weeks. Her hair was a mess, and it looked as if she was recovering from a punch to the jaw.

In her hand was a .357 revolver.

I skidded to a halt when I saw her, but it was too late. We were all pinned by the narrowness of the alley. We were directly in her gun sights.

Jackson

No. Oh, God, no.

"Kayla," I said as calmly as I could, "please put down the gun."

"You bastard," she said pointing the gun directly at me.

That's right, focus on me. Leave them out of it.

"You fucking bastard. You took everything. I loved him, damn it, and you took him away from me."

Her hands were shaking badly. She was very unstable.

"Why couldn't you just buy the fucking company? You had plenty of money? Don't you know how hard I worked on that? It was going to be our ideal life. We were going to run off to Mexico. He was going to marry me." The tears were streaming freely down her cheeks. She was absolutely hysterical.

"Kayla, we can work this out. Just put the gun down..."

"No, you fucking prick," she screamed, "I am done working things out with you. You never gave a rat's ass about my opinion. It's always been your way or the highway." She was moving closer to me, her eyes fixed on mine. I needed to keep her focus on me.

I saw Mark shifting his stance out of the corner of my eye, and I hoped he was doing what I thought he was doing.

"That's not true, Kayla. I value your opinion."

Stay with me. Focus all that hate right here.

"Liar. You fucking liar!" She was still advancing on me. "You cost me the love of my life, my future, my dreams. Everything!"

How had I let it get this bad? She was completely insane. She was going to kill us all.

I could barely understand her. Her words were broken and tortured.

"And now... now... I am going to take from you what you took from me."

She turned away from me and pointed the gun at Alissa, I tried to block her path, but Mark was faster. He had drawn his gun slowly as she spoke, and when she turned to aim at Alissa, he shot Kayla twice, squarely in the chest. The gunshots echoed loudly in the small alley. Kayla fell to the ground in a heap. Her gun clattered to the pavement.

The policemen who had been stationed at the front of the building ran around the corner yelling into their radios about an ambulance. Alissa buried her face in my chest. I had never been so glad to hold her. I realized how close I had come to losing her.

"Shhh, baby," I soothed, "It's over. It's all over now."

Mark went into cop mode, and the excitement swirled around us. Kayla was pronounced dead at the scene by the paramedics. Mark handled the statements and other police matters. We were all shaken up, but virtually unharmed.

The truck driver was found in the back of the hijacked truck, duct tapped to one of Alissa's new chairs. I felt terrible about the mess I'd involved him in, but he was amazingly understanding. I had my lawyers provide him with a settlement. They found a legal loophole, which allowed me to compensate him if he agreed not to talk to the press. I didn't care about the legal jargon; I just wanted to make sure that he didn't need to drive truck any more if he didn't want to. He deserved some time off.

Later that evening, Alissa finally got her furniture moved

in. It wasn't properly arranged, but we could do that tomorrow. The truck needed to get back to its rightful place, and we all just wanted to be done with it. Enough was enough for one day. I was exhausted once again. I wanted nothing more than to take her home with me and fall asleep with her in my arms.

I got a terrible sinking feeling in my stomach. What if she didn't want to come home with me? Kayla was dead, and the danger was gone. There was no longer a reason for her to stay with me.

I was suddenly very insecure. What if she didn't want me any more at all? I had involved her in a living nightmare, and now that it was over, she would be smart to just walk away.

"What are you frowning about?"

I looked up. Alissa was standing in the doorway, silhouetted by the kitchen light with her hands on her hips. She was so lovely.

"Nothing," I said. I didn't sound convincing, even to myself. "I was just thinking I would head home."

Her forehead wrinkled. She looked as heartbroken as I felt. Maybe she wanted to come after all.

"I mean..." I backtracked, "unless you needed something else, er if, I mean..." *Geez Hayes, could you sound like any more of an inarticulate ass?* "Alissa, I would like for you to come home with me, again... I mean... if you want to..."

She smiled, and I thought I would die of happiness right there in her restaurant.

"I was kinda' hoping that maybe you would like to stay here tonight?" she asked shyly. "I mean, since it's safe and all now? I know it's not as nice as your place, but..."

I hadn't even thought of that, but I was thrilled. I was going to get to experience a night in the life of Alissa Allen, sleep in her sheets, surrounded by her smell. I couldn't think of one thing that I would like to do more.

"That sounds great. I'll just run home for a minute, if

that's okay, to get some clothes, change cars, and take care of a couple of little things. I'll come right back?"

She ambled across the restaurant to me. "Don't keep me waiting, Hayes." Her smile was breathtaking. I wanted to see that playful look over and over and over again.

"I wouldn't dream of making you wait."

Exhaustion and Abundance

Jackson

I ran home as quickly as possible and grabbed an overnight bag. I felt grimy after everything that had happened, and I wanted a shower, but I was hoping I could talk Alissa into showering with me. Thoughts of running my hands all over her soapy skin had me racing even faster through my apartment.

I took the Audi back to her place. I hated to leave the Vanquish out of the garage overnight.

Mark was just walking out the front door as I pulled up. I hadn't had a chance to thank him, and I wanted to rectify that oversight.

"Mark," I called, as I jogged across the street to him. "I, um, I just wanted to say thank you... for today. Your daughter is one of the best things that has ever happened to me, and I don't know what I would do if I lost her. I can't tell you how grateful I am that you were there, in that alley."

"That girl *is* the best thing that ever happened to me, Jackson. I am very proud to be her father, and I am proud of you for doing what you did today, too."

There was an awkward emotional pause for a moment while neither one of us knew what to say. I studied my shoelaces. Mark shifted his weight around.

"But don't let it go to your head kid," Mark finally joked, "I still don't trust you with her." He gave me a smile that said I was okay in his book, and then he slapped me on the back. As he walked away, I ran back to my car and got my stuff.

Alissa let me in and then locked up behind me. I dropped my bag and grabbed her unexpectedly.

"Come here you," I said, grabbing her around the waist. She jumped into my arms and wrapped her legs around me.

I backed her up to one of the new tables and sat her ass down on the edge. "Want to break in the new furniture?" I asked, before sucking her bottom lip into my mouth.

She chuckled. "I doubt my customers would appreciate that."

"You're probably right," I sighed, "and truthfully I would like a shower more than anything. It's been quite a day."

"A shower sounds lovely," she agreed. I picked up my bag. Ten minutes later she was leaning back against my chest, wearing nothing but bubbles. I gently traced her hip bones with my fingertips and enjoyed the feel of her soft skin under the water. Granted, Alissa's tub was not really designed for two people, but we managed. I made a mental note to do this again in a larger tub.

We talked about the day, and I vented my fears and frustrations to her. I was worried about Robert and whether I should allow him to remain on my board. I was worried about Nick and Ryan and if they would be convicted. I was worried that Jason wouldn't be able to smooth this over with the press.

I was also worried about Alissa and if she would leave me now that the danger and excitement were over. I did not voice this last concern, however. To say it aloud would bring it to life, and I was too much a coward for that. Apparently, Alissa was braver than me.

"Jackson?"

"Yes, dear?"

I could feel her smile as she turned her head against my chest.

"I just..." she hesitated. "I know that we really haven't known each other very long, but I kinda feel like we've been through a lot together already."

"I couldn't agree more. In fact, I'm hoping for quieter times to come, at least for a little while."

"Yeah. I'll be glad to get back to normal, but I'm a little worried about something."

"What's that?"

"Well, I really do appreciate everything you've done for me lately, but I'm afraid that I'm going to lose you now that you no longer need to be my guardian superhero." I opened my mouth to speak, but she continued. "My heart is invested now, and it's going to hurt a lot if you leave."

Oh, thank God.

I wrapped my arms around her and pulled her back against my chest, holding her as tightly as I could without hurting her. I brushed my lips against her neck right below her ear.

"Alissa Allen, I never want to hear you say anything so ridiculous again. My heart is invested, too, and I am not going anywhere. You are stuck with me for the rest of eternity as far as I am concerned."

"Eternity huh?" she turned to face me, and I kissed her gently. "That's a long time."

"Not long enough," I replied, and I meant it. I could never grow tired of this woman. We sat in a comfortable silence for a while longer, but the water was cooling quickly, and I wanted to be in a warm bed with her instead.

A few minutes later, I had Alissa towel dried and tucked into bed beside me. We leisurely explored each other's bodies and made love slowly, whispering words of endearment that never meant more. Eventually, we fell asleep with our limbs tangled together and our hearts entwined.

I had never felt more at peace, despite the trying day. It was like I had finally found my home. Wherever Alissa was, that's where home would be.

Alissa

I woke around 7:00 the next morning to a disappointingly empty bed. After such an amazing night, I had wanted to wake up beside Jackson, but I knew that he had a lot of work to do. He left a note, folded into a delicate origami bird, on the bedside table. Origami? Was there anything that man couldn't do?

I pushed aside my feelings of inadequacy. Jackson told me last night very clearly that he was serious about being with me. I was going to trust his words.

I smiled as I read the note.

> My Dearest Alissa,
>
> I can't tell you what torture it was to leave your warm bed for a cold office. I hope you'll forgive my absence and allow me to return this evening... and every evening. I'll think of you twice a second until then.
>
> With love,
>
> Jackson

With love...

I rolled out of bed and made my way downstairs. I was completely incapable of keeping the ridiculous smile off of my face.

I made some coffee and then set to work arranging my new

tables and chairs. I would reopen the restaurant tomorrow, and I had a lot to do before then.

Tyler came over around lunchtime to help me sort out the food situation and get everything ready. We started by going through the kitchen. I bought many of my ingredients fresh daily, but we always had a lot of food in the place. We hadn't been open for three days, and some of it wasn't going to be good for much longer. I had very high standards when it came to quality, so I wasn't going to use them when we re-opened, but I always hated to throw food away.

We started cooking, and I easily fell into a comfortable pattern, like I always did. I had really missed my kitchen, so much in fact, that I might have gotten a little carried away.

....Okay, I got really carried away. When we were done, we had a massive amount of food ranging from sandwiches to full dinners to baked goods. I had no idea what we were going to do with it all.

We packed everything back in the fridge as a temporary solution. We were going to have to get rid of it today so that I could bring in all of the new groceries before tomorrow morning.

I called Jackson. I told myself that I was calling because he might have a good idea for what to do with the food, but if I was honest with myself I knew I just wanted an excuse to talk to him. I was such a sap.

I rang his cell. He picked up after the first ring.

"Alissa?"

"Hi, Jackson."

"I miss you." I could hear the smile in his voice. I was glad I called.

"I miss you, too. Are you busy?"

"Yeah, kind of, but I have time for you. What's up?"

"Right, um Tyler and I did some cooking to make room for the new groceries that I am going to buy today, and now we have a ton of food and no one to eat it. Do you know anyone who might want it?"

"How much food is a ton?"

"Oh, about forty dinners..."

"Really?"

"Well, yeah, and I needed to use up the sliced meats so we made some sandwiches... and some other things..." When I said it out loud, it suddenly seemed like a ridiculous amount of food.

"Alissa? How much food are we really talking about?"

"Well maybe fifty or so sandwiches, too... And a couple pots of soup... And some baked goods... Tyler made pies to use up the berries – they were getting moldy, Jackson. I can't have that."

I suddenly felt the need to explain my random cooking spree. I don't care what his note said. I made massive amounts of food for no one. He was going to think that I was nuts.

"I just... well... I got to cooking, and I've kinda' been missing the kitchen. Please don't think I'm crazy. I really did need to use this stuff up."

He laughed into the phone, and it was the most wonderful sound. "I don't think you're crazy, and I have an idea for where we can send the food."

"Really?"

"Really. Let me make some calls, and then I'll come over and help you deliver it. I have a quick 4:00 meeting, and then I'll be over. You can do your shopping now if you want, and then we'll put the old food in your van and bring in the new food. Sound like a plan?"

"Perfect. Thank you, Jackson."

"You're welcome. See you soon."

I felt better knowing that we would have somewhere to send the leftover food. Tyler came with me to get the new supplies. I usually shopped alone, but I needed the extra help for a full kitchen re-stock. I could manage the market in the morning, but I needed things like potatoes, which came in fifty pound bags that were a pain.

Two hours later, Tyler and I returned with a van full of food to find Jackson leaning against my kitchen door. He was talking to someone on the phone. He looked happy, and I hoped that I might be a small part of the reason why.

When I got out of the van, he announced that Jason and Ben were coming to help us with the food. The plan was to take the hot meals and soups to a church that had a soup kitchen. They would be served as part of dinner the next day. The sandwiches were going to a shelter tonight, the same shelter that Jackson had stayed in just a short week ago. I asked if I would need more food. I was willing to put together some extra sandwiches if we wouldn't have enough, but Jackson said that fifty was perfect. He'd also picked up a couple of cases of bottled water to go with the sandwiches.

We took all of the food to donate out and brought all of the new stuff in for tomorrow. Jason and Ben followed my van in Jason's Jeep. We went to the church first and loaded the food into the refrigerators there. We were just going to leave the pots and trays. I could pick them up tomorrow.

We arrived at the shelter about twenty minutes before the men would be allowed inside. The staff let us in the back entrance, and we set up just inside the front doors. The plan was to hand each person who wanted one, a sandwich and a water on their way to find a bunk. Jackson and I stood side by side, armed with food and water, and Jason and Ben took the other side so we could have two lines.

I will never forget the look on Jackson's face as he handed my simple sandwiches to those men. He was clearly humbled, and he seemed truly grateful for the opportunity to serve. It was clear that he preferred being on this side of the line this time, but I thought that Jackson would probably have a lot more experiences like this one in the future. He'd learned something about what it means to be hungry, and he'd learned that there are more important things in life than working hard all of the time. I thought Jackson would probably be more of a hands-on giver from now on.

Jason looked up at one point and winked at me. It was obvious that he was very proud of his brother. I was proud of him, too, not to mention madly in love with him.

The sandwiches were mostly gone in about ten minutes, so we packed up and headed back to my restaurant. Jason took the leftovers with him, saying that six or seven sandwiches would be no match for a guy like him. We all laughed at that, but something told me it was probably true.

Jackson and I spent the rest of the night drinking wine on my couch and talking about everything that crossed our minds. It would become a frequent habit of ours for years to come. It was the start of an incredible relationship.

Epilogue

One Year Later

Jackson Hayes, the brilliant real estate tycoon, entrepreneur, financial genius, and recently married man was walking home from work. Admittedly, this was a rare event prompted by the early springtime weather coupled with an extremely productive late-afternoon meeting.

He was in the process of purchasing a company owned by none other than Mr. Matt Ozwell, former part-time employee to Mrs. Alissa Allen-Hayes. It was a small chain of sporting goods stores that were surprisingly profitable despite their new CEO's lazy attitude.

Matt had inherited the company from his father a month ago, when he'd graduated from college, and Jackson wanted to buy it before Matt had a chance to really screw it up. The due diligence checked out, and pending any further information, the deal was scheduled to close in less than thirty days.

Jackson loosened his tie and threw his perfectly tailored jacket over his arm for the hike across town. He was whistling as he walked, and daydreaming about his incredible wife, Alissa.

About a half a block up, he saw group of three teenage boys harassing an older man that was sitting on the cement steps in front of a vacant retail building. He watched the scene for a moment debating the right thing to do.

The man had a plastic cup in one hand and he was holding it up in an effort to shield himself as the boys flicked pennies at him. The man was making no aggressive move to defend himself, but three against one was not good odds, and the man didn't appear to be in the best health.

"Hey!" Jackson yelled coming closer and attracting attention to the boys. "Knock it off!"

The boys looked at him and seemed to realize that he wasn't kidding. They took of running down the street leaving only a string of profanities in their wake.

"You okay?" Jackson asked the man.

"Yes, thank you. They're only boys. Their parents don't raise them right any more."

Jackson nodded in agreement before putting a twenty-dollar bill in the man's cup and going on his way. After several visits to volunteer at the shelters, he knew that twenty dollars would not solve the man's problems, but it might feed him for a day or two.

As he was walking away, his phone vibrated in his pocket.

"Hello."

"What's up my brother?" Jason's boisterous voice echoed through the phone.

"Nothing."

"Good, we're having a night out. Shel, Lexy, and 'Lissa are off at some open house thing, and you know I can't cook for shit. We're going down to the Phyrst. David and I will meet you there in half an hour."

The line went dead. Jackson looked up at the street sign. He was still ten blocks from home, and it was a ten-minute drive from home to the bar. It looked like he'd need that cab after all.

Jackson

"..so then Matt tries to tell me that living in the wild is tough," I said. Jason chuckled and shook his head, taking a long swig of his beer. "And then, when I call him on it, he tells me that I wouldn't survive one week in the wilderness on my own, unless I bought a ton of his camping gear."

I paused while the waitress set our burgers in front of us. "This looks so good. I was freaking starving."

Jason was still shaking his head and laughing across the table. "He's right though," he said.

"Who's right?" I asked.

"Matt Ozwell. Wilderness survival sucks. I sure as hell wouldn't want to try it."

"What?" I paused with my burger halfway to my mouth. "You don't think I could do it?"

I looked at David, who just shrugged and returned his attention to his fries.

Jason smiled his typical huge goofy smile at me, and I knew I was in trouble. "No, I don't," he said. "I've got $50,000 that says you can't last one week in the wild." He was cracking up laughing.

"What?" Not this again. David was laughing and shaking his head, clearly trying to stay out of this bit of brother bonding time.

"You heard me," Jason said. "I'll bet you fifty grand that you don't make it one week in the woods. Hell, I'll even let you have a tent!"

"You can't be fucking serious," I said. "I'm a newlywed. 'Lissa will kick my ass!"

"Take Alissa with you," he said. "When was the last time you two had an adventure together? It'll be a marriage builder. If I remember correctly, it worked out okay for you two the last time we tried this kinda' thing."

I looked back to David. "What do you think, Dave?"

"I think I'm staying as far away from this as I can. Lexy will kill me if she finds out that I had a hand in making Alissa spend a week in the woods."

I laughed at that. Lexy could be quite a handful. David was a smart man to stay on her good side, but Jason was right. Alissa and I both worked a lot, and we didn't get to spend as much time together as I would like. We hadn't even taken a honeymoon yet – preferring to wait until the ongoing legal matters were all solved.

Nick's trial had just wrapped up last week. He got thirty years for kidnapping, assault with a deadly weapon, embezzlement, and a whole list of other charges. I was so relieved to have the whole mess behind us, and I knew Alissa was, too.

My businesses had settled down again with a new board member to replace Kayla. She was doing fabulously in her new role. The investigation into Robert had determined that he made a bad judgment call, but was not maliciously involved in anyway. He was doing his job a little more cautiously now, but was actually performing better than ever. The press had lost interest, as they always do, and we were back to business as usual.

Maybe it was time to move on to the next great adventure. Alissa was an incredible woman; she would understand.

"Deal," I said. "Fifty thousand dollars says Alissa and I are perfectly fine after living one week in the wild."

Author's Notes

Thank you so much for reading. I really hope that you've enjoyed Billionaire. It was truly a blast to write and a joy to share.

Despite the blatant set up in the epilogue, I do not have plans to write a squeal at this time. Never say never though - maybe some day.

This is the first novel that I've made an attempt at marketing, but it is not the only one that I've written, so if you'd like to see more you can reach me at kdfleeger@gmail.com. I'd love to hear from you.

There are a lot of people who have been a huge help in producing this work. I would like to thank my amazing husband for putting up with my compulsive writing spells, and my parents who first taught me to love reading and writing. Thank you also to LskNH and Twilighter456 who read and encouraged this story when it was in its online infancy. Special thanks to the whole fanfiction community for reading and commenting. I am always amazed at the generosity and thoughtfulness of those who read and write simply because they love fiction.

I hope to see you again in the future.

K. D. Fleeger

About the Author

Ms. Fleeger lives in Pittsburgh, Pennsylvania with her husband and two cats. She has a full time career as a marketing director in the commercial real estate industry, but can be frequently found writing for the shear joy of writing in her spare time.

She also enjoys traveling, camping, and down-hill snow skiing. Her favorite authors include Stephen King, Fannie Flagg, Stephanie Meyer, J. K. Rowling and Henery David Thoreau.